Not Always A Happy Ending

Part II: The Past

notionpress
.com

Not Always A Happy Ending

Part II: The Past

Shriyut Kumar Srivastava

notionpress.com

Notion Press

Old No. 38, New No. 6

McNichols Road, Chetpet

Chennai - 600 031

First Published by Notion Press 2016

ISBN 978-93-5206-691-9

For my Sister

Contents

Acknowledgements

Once again, the time has come to appreciate the people who have supported me through the worst of times, believed in me when I was losing hope and helped me get to this point.

Of course, nothing I do is ever complete without thanking my wonderful parents – architect Umesh Kumar – my father and Dr. ManishaSrivastava – my mother. I sometimes wonder how I am so blessed to be called your son. Everyone experiences hard times, but the way we come out it, is what matters. And you have helped me conquer every problem, no matter how hard it seemed to me. The pain I go through, the work I have to do, all of it feels paid off when I see your proud smiles. And I promise I'll do anything to keep that happiness in your eyes and the pride on your faces.

My amazing little sister, Shriya, has been the silent critic in my life. Her expressions have been enough to tell me if I am on the right path. Not a lot of people like me, but even they know that I love my sister more than anything else in this world. You are the most special person in my life and every moment that I've made you laugh is the best in my life. Thank you for correcting my mistakes and helping me become a better person. My books, achievements and the person I am, nothing was possible without you.

Prakhar, Aafreen, Mekhla, Ashmita, Shagun, Anvi, Shanker, Anupam and Manjari, without all of you, this book would not have happened. I know I am an impossible person to deal with and of course, most of you have a lot of issues with me. But I do appreciate everything you did to make me reach this place where I am right now. Thank you for helping me in every way you could in my worst times and taking care of me when I needed it the most.

Sonali and Altamash; you are the two people closest to me in my life. The job of being my best friend comes with a lot of responsibilities and issues; that is why everyone runs away. But the two of you know me the way nobody ever does and you stood by me when I had lost all the will to continue to fight; telling me, "You're still here, you can go further." I know that our relationship is not something where we appreciate each other openly; but I'm sure that both of you know how much love, respect, trust and gratitude I have in my heart for you, for keeping me up and not letting me fall. You have worked hard to mold me into the strong person I've become. I promise that you will forever be rewarded with my attention and affection.

A special thanks tomy four grandparents. Just having you in my life is enough. I feel blessed that I was born in your family and the amount of love you have given me is indescribable. And it's really important to mention my little cousins: Divyansh, Satvik, Aadya and Dhruvi. I wish a better world for you to live in, full of people with beautiful hearts and honest souls. You are too young to understand anything that is written here, but I hope that whenever you finally read this book, you feel that skip in your heartbeat that I wish you to feel.

My publishers, Notion Press – it was serendipitythat I came across your website, but it was for the best. I am extremely grateful to you and proud that I am a part of the Notion Press family.

And of course, thank you to everyone who have read and loved the first part of this trilogy. Making a 'not always a happy ending' trilogy was a risk that paid off because of the trust you had in my writing and the love you showered me with, after reading the first part. I promise to get better with time.

Lastly, thanking everyone who made my life miserable,akin to a living hell, is really important. Thank you for doing your best to make me give up.It only made me a better person. I might still not know what true love or a pure soul is. But I surely know what it isn't and that was not possible without the atrociously dreadful-hearted people who I came across while working on this book.

Introduction

This is my favorite part – I get to present the book from my side. I still can't believe that time has passed so quickly. I remember when I was working on the first part of the trilogy, wishing it to be good enough for people to beg for the second part… Thankfully that's exactly what happened. The immense love I received was overwhelming. And I pray the same for this second part.

2015 has been the worst year of my entire existence for numerous reasons. I went through emotional, physical and mental torture. And one person was responsible for all of it – me! My decisions, my beliefs and my naïveté were the reasons I was not happy. But it led me to enlightenment about happiness,that it is no different from sadness. Both are addictive in their own ways. And most importantly, a happy person wants to be happy and a depressed person finds solace in despondency. I found my solace, my serenity in darkness and it was beautiful.

I had to do everything in my power to make this book better than the first part and I sincerely hope it is. It was a really hard job to do because of the way the first part was appreciated.

It's now been three years of me existing with the characters of this trilogy living inside my mind; especially Jay and Estella. Jay influences my personal life and Estella makes me have faith in a beautiful future. I'm 66% done with the series, only one book is left and it's surely going to be heartbreaking to let these characters go.

Now let's finally start with this book. As you may have smartly guessed and because I made it so obvious that it is the story of Jay Malhotra's past,it will answer all your questions about his present condition. It introduces the characters of Viola and Amelia who are exquisite in their own ways. The words in this book are stunning. Jay Malhotra has a glorious way with words and the way he presents his thoughts… it's just marvelous. It truly will be fascinating for you when the events of the first book and the second one connect. Just a suggestion, do not judge the decisions a character takes. Everyone has a different way of thinking.

If I have to describe the book, I'd say it's a little less confusing than the first one as it is written with the purpose of providing clarity to the readers. I've tried to carefully juxtapose black and white themes. Some pages are full of the realest kind of love and some may silence your mind with their depth and depression. The changes are – it's darker, more romantic and more intense. But it's as intriguing as the first part was. You will again be driven crazy, waiting for the third part – the epic finale.

In the end, I would just say, all the best; it is going to be a roller coaster read about love and its dark side, I promise. Of course, not everyone will agree with my thinking regarding love and destiny. Some may raise stupid arguments because that's how they are. But as the author, I'd suggest that you put your beliefs and thinking aside and immerse yourself in the lives of the characters. Trust me, nothing is better than that. And I really hope you lovereading it as much as I loved writing it.

PS: The finale is waiting for you.

Prologue

"Hence, I'm coming to you in a minute, but can't stop me from asking you this question right now. I love you Estella Aurora Hudson. So, will you…" Before Agastya could complete the words, there was the loud sound of a truck slipping and everyone saw it rolling towards him.

"AGASTYA!" Estella yelled at the top of her lungs as she saw the truck crushing the love of her life. Her heart was in her mouth. She ran and so did the people around – everyone ran as fast as they could to reach him. "No Agastya!!" Estella was shouting as she ran, tears gushing from her eyes. Her heel broke and she fell. When she got up,she found it hard to run,for she hadsprained her leg. But she continued running without caring about anything other than her man.

A group of people pulled the truck driver and Agastya out of the rubble. Estellakneeled down to him and held him in her arms.

"You can't leave me Agastya! Please don't leave me baby please I'm begging you." She started weeping while Agastya's blood flowed into the red color of her dress.

Agastya and the driverwere rushed to the nearest hospital. There were no tears left to cry anymore but that didn't stop Estella from sobbing.

"Estella, everything will be okay I swear." Kathryn and Laurel arrived as soon as they could, to support their friend.

They tried to hug her but she was just too horrified, that she didn't want anyone else to touch her but her Agastya.

"I think she needs a little space," Laurel said to Kathryn as they looked at her, shaking with fear. They hadn't told Estella that they had just gotten engaged.

Estella was anxious to know what was happening to her boyfriend. The distress and horror were making her heart feel weak. The most important element of her existence, the center of her universe, was fighting for his life. If she could, she would give her life at that moment just to save his. Her hands were joined together; her eyes were closed, and lips were continuously praying to every God that exists in the universe, to not let her be without her Agastya. She loved him; she needed him.

The doctor came out of the ICU and Estella's heart stopped for a second. She knew by hisexpression that he was not bringing good news, but she just couldn't stop thinking optimistically. She and her friends rushed towards him to ask if Agastya was okay.

"Ms. Hudson." The doctor paused, seeing Estella's condition. Her eyeliner was smudged and had smeared her cheeks because of her weeping. Her dress had blood on it and she was finding it hard to stand up properly because of her sprained leg. But nothing mattered to her other than her Agastya's health.

"Yes doctor? He's okay? Not a major injury, right? Don't worry; we'll be careful next time when we go out." Her optimism spoke. "Please get some juice for him Kat." She smiled at Kathryn while her tears slid down her cheeks. Both her friends were crying as they knew that she was just trying to cope, with positivity.

"I'm sorry Ms. Hudson." The doctor patted her shoulder. "We did everything we could."

Estella died with her Agastya. She just looked at the doctor, trying her best not to lose her mind. She clumsily wiped her tears off and gave a smile. "It's okay. I don't think he would need that juice after all." She looked at her friends and held their hands. "Can I…see him…please?" It was getting difficult for her to say anything else.

"Sure." The doctor instructed a nurse to take her to Agastya.

She entered the room and there he was, lying peacefully. She could see his face held that unintentional innocent smile that he used to give her whenever he felt romantic. She went close to him and held his injured hand. His whole body was in an awful shape with cuts and injuries all over, because of the accident. But for Estella, that man would always be perfect.

"Agu, baby. Please get up my love." She started crying. "I love you so much. I'm begging you, please get up and hug me tightly. I need you to hold me baby! Please tell me this is all a dream and not real. Please Agastya. PLEASE AGASTYA!" She yelled.

"AGASTYA!" Estella opened her eyes suddenly, breaking out of her nightmare. She sat up and wiped off the tears in her eyes. Almost every night, she dreamt of that moment, since it happened.

She got out of bed and went into the bathroom. She looked in the mirror and her Agastya's words, "Look in the mirror without shedding a tear." came to her mind. And she didn't cry. There was not much left in her that she could cry. For the past threemonths, tears would just leave her eyes, but she would be okay; exceptfor thenight before.

Estella made coffee for herself in Agastya's cup. She had been living at his apartment since his passing. She went tothe balcony and sipped the coffee, while thinking about all that Aarav had told her about Jay.

'How could a person go through so much and still carry on talking about love?' she thought to herself. Suddenly her phone beeped. It was a text from Aarav.

'I would urge you not to talk anything about what I told you to Jay. He's already very angry with me. He hasn't even come back yet,'the text read.

'Oh yeah, I won't. And don't worry; I'm sure he'll be back soon. Besides it's Saturday. No university today.' She replied and got back to her thoughts of Jay and what Aarav told her about him. She was so confused when he had taken that name. 'Viola Harris.'

(11 hours ago)

Estella paused after listening to Aarav's words. "What? Who is Viola Harris?" she asked him in a confused tone.

Till that moment, Aarav's mind had see-sawed back to not telling her and he was trying to calm himself down. "Did I say that name? I didn't mean to. It's just one random name. I was…" She stopped him in between his nervous rambling.

"Look Aarav, I don't want to know. It's his personal matter and it's wrong for me to know anything without his permission." She wiped her tears and stood up. "I've to go back home. You were right, this was a mistake." She tried to look for her bag.

Aarav stopped her "No Estella, wait." He requested her to sit down again. "Look, I don't know why, but I just feel that it is Jay's or my responsibility to tell you the reason why he behaved the way he did. You are going to spend a lot of time with him and you deserve to know. It's important, but it's not easy to do that. So just, bear with me." He took out his phone and showed Estella a picture. "I saw Jay writing this a few days ago. Read it. I know you say you don't want to know anything, but after this you will."

Estella looked steadily at Aarav. "Give it to me." She took the phone and started reading.

I know I'm capable
Of killing my feelings
This soul feels unattainable
With no sign of healing.

It all makes me want someone
Who could just numb my pain
As currently no one can earn
My trust and make me sane.

Make no mistake, I don't need love;
Only my palette needs cleansing.
No amount of bliss from spirits above
Can hurt the demon within menacing.

You could try your best to fix me,
But with time you'll gradually see;
That I am an animal; just want the meat;
And you will never reduce this heat.

Jay's words were shattering; especially because Estella was experiencing the same feelings for the last three months. After a minute of thinking, she finally gave in to Aarav. "Okay Aarav. But first, who was this Viola?"

"No Estella; that is actually not the beginning. If I am telling this to you, you need to know everything. Who is Jay, who is Amelia and of course, Viola." He took a deep breath. "It all started in SAU, seven years ago. It was not that big a deal to get admission there. There was no Professor Jay then." He smiled in the hope that Estella would smile as well. But she was quiet and did not respond. Aarav took another deep breath and started his story.

Chapter – 1

Once Upon a Summer

[Summer '07]

Life was good. I mean, seriously, amazing; my own pad with no one to say a thing to me.Mini bar, Italian marble, PlayStation attached to a huge 50 inch TV, king sized beds in two rooms and state-of-the-art bathroom. It was not a house. It was heaven.During my Bachelor's I had to stay home with my parents but it was just awesome since I came to SAU for my MBA.

For one year, it was all clear blue skies and smooth sails. But then, my stupid friends decided to have a stupid party at my place and my stupid neighbors complained to the stupid police about stupid noise; and now my stupid parents want me to have a stupid flat mate so I wouldn't be able to enjoy and my life would be hell. I suggested that they let any of my friends move in with me but, "No Aarav they're a bad influence on you. We'll choose someone for you."

"Aarav Mehta is about to have a boyfriend." My friends would laugh at me. I didn't know why I still hung out with them. I so know that they just use me because my parents have money and they can fulfill their wishes with the money my parents give me; especially after that bizarre, unreal evening.

The doorbell finally rang. Apparently my father had chosen this guy to be my flat mate. It was surprising that my father talked more about him after meeting him just once, than he did about me in a year. I didn't even remember his name; I guess it was Shriyut or something.

I looked in the mirror to put my scary face on. I had to do something to keep him away from my Aarav-pad.

I opened the door in the coldest way possible. He looked like Ted Mosby from How I Met Your Mother. "Heh. Nerd." I said to myself.

"You must be Aarav. I've heard a lot about you from your father. I'm Shriyut." He shook my hand with a smile. Okay, he didn't seem scared. That was catastrophic.

"Sup Shriyut." It was time for plan B: showing the cool side. I invited him in and sat him down so that he couldadmire my amazing place. I don't know why, but whenever I looked at him I felt like we had met before. Was he my destiny? Were my friends dead-on when they called my new flat mate my boyfriend?

"No," he said with a smile.

"No I swear I know they were just joking and it was just a random thought in my mind. I'm not that kind of guy," I panicked.

"I said no tothe vodka that you are offering me. What are you talking about?" I hadautomatically offered him a drink. Force of habit I guess.

"Nothing," I tried to save my dignity. "It's a part of a play I'm rehearsing for." Nailed it! "So Shruyeet, right?" I intentionally pronouncedhis name wrong.

"Uh no, it's Shriyut. You said it right twominutes ago." He seemed annoyed. And so was I.

"Yeah sure; look you can't stay here. It's not the place for you. I don't care what my father told you but you're a problem for my 'Euphoriaarav'," I told him straight.

"What on earth is 'Euphoriaarav'? No, never mind! It's fine. I'll leave don't worry. Sorry I bothered you." Those words rang in my ears as if I had won a championship belt. If my father forced me to get a flat mate I'd get any of my friends, change their name when theymet my parents, and then it'll all work out smoothly.

"Sorry to waste your time. You have a beautiful place," Shriyut told me as he started to pick up his stuff. Oh, the sip of vodka after reclaimingyour house is amazing. I looked at him as he picked up the shattered pieces of his dreams and I realized that this bastard that I had become, it wasn't me. I had never been this way; it was all the influence I was in that made me be that awful way.

"Hey Shriyut, wait!" I stopped him. "Look, you can stay here. It's just that…" He cut me in between.

"I understand. Sometimes parents can get weird. You have nothing to feel bad about." He smiled and just then I knew that he was really a good person.

I don't know what was in him but I could see our friendship going far. Especially because he was a great cook. "Yes dad, he's here." It was like my dad was fixing us up to get married. Not even the police asked so many questions when I was arrested, than my father asking me about Shriyut being comfortable at my place.

"Your parents are really nice." he said to me as he cooked a Spanish omelet for me.

"They can sometimes be a couple of 'Aarav-eating' zombies but yeah, they're nice," I said as I looked at my wallpaper of them. "What about your parents? Where do they live?" I asked him and I could suddenly see him losing his smile.

"They died in a car accident. Do you like black pepper?" He instantly changed the topic. It was a bit embarrassing to see him be so uneasy but I knew now to not talk about his parents.

"This is really good. Really very good man! Oh you're so not leaving this house!" I told him as I shoved big bites into my mouth.

"Oh thank you so much," he laughed. "Now that I'll be living here for quite a while, let me get some more of my things and I'll be back in an hour."

"Of course and hey…" He turned back to me.

"Yeah?"

"I'm happy you're here." He smiled.

"So am I." And he made me smile.

Everything went better without my plan being involved. He was a nice person. And most importantly, he was real. He wasn't like those jerks whohide information just to live at my place. I know I wasn't the most perfect host when he first arrived, but I never have been a bad person and I'll give Shriyut reasons to like me too.

On the other side, my new flat mate was happy too. He finally had a place close to the university and a great view of the Reindeer Gardens.

He was putting his bags in the taxi when a girl came up to him from behind and touched his shoulder.

"Excuse me? Do you have a second?" He turned back and recognized her immediately.

"Oh hey, you're the girl from that night," he said to her with a smile. "How are you now?"

"I'm perfectly fine. I just saw you here and came to thank you for that night. You have no idea how much my friends and I appreciated your help. If you hadn't been there I don't know what could havehappened." She smiled and gave him a quick kiss on his cheek. "Thank you so much." They both were red with shyness.

"I should thank you." He paused for a second. "I'm sorry, where are my manners, I'm…" She cut him in between.

"The amazing Jay Malhotra; I know." She smiled and kept shaking his hand without saying a word.

"And you are?" Jay asked with a laugh.

"Oh yes, hi. I'm Amelia. Amelia Prentiss," she replied.

[The Present]

There are different kinds of drugs – cocaine, heroin, marijuana, love, depression, guilt. Jay Malhotra was high on one of these drugs – guilt. He kept telling himself that his reactionsof the night before were justified, but deep down he knew he had done wrong to Estella. Especially after what Kathryn and Laurel had told him about her recent tragedy.

Every step towards his home made him feel worse. He just wanted to run somewhere. A place where no one would judge him for the way he was. The guard outside his place was surprised to see his condition. His wrinkled shirt was poorly tucked, he had a bottle of whiskey in his pants' pocket and his tie was gone.

"What?" Jay irritatingly asked the guard, dragging his blazer behind him.

His question broke the guard's stare. "No sir, nothing sir." He hesitated. "Do you want any help sir?"

"I'm fine." Jay grunted and went up to the elevator.

Everyone in the apartment had heard the commotion. Therefore,whoever saw him couldn't help but stare. Jay was used to people staring at him, but for the first time, those eyes were scaring him. He kept calm but he was horrified.

He reached his door and took a deep breath. His guilt regarding Estella was eating him up. 'How could I be such a monster? I am not this person. I never have been this way! What is wrong with you Jay?' He kept talking to himself as he opened the door.

Wherever he looked, he saw the damage he had caused the night before. Pieces of the broken lamps, the wrecked TV and wasted food were all over the place. Jay's blazer slipped out of his arm, onto the ground. His hands were shivering with remorse and he let go. He closed the door and embraced his tears. The last he had cried was when Amelia had died. But lately, tears were on an overflow.He hugged his knees with his arms and cried his eyes out. Even he knew that repeating, 'I'm not a bad person' would not change the things that had happened; but it didn't stop him from shouting those words at the top of his lungs.

Unexpectedly, he heard that little melody on his piano that "she" used to play.He quickly looked and there she was again, wearing his favorite dress. He smiled but it did not take him much to realize that she wasn't real. He wanted to throw something at her but he loved her. After all that had happened, after all that he had suffered, after all those times he had told Aarav he hated her, he still loved her.

He stopped crying and stood up. As it had happened before as well, he walked towards her like he was hypnotized. "I missed this music," he said as he sat down beside her.

"I would play, but you stopped cleaning the piano babe," she said with a smile.

"I missed the music, but I didn't want you to play; not this 'you' anyway." He kissed the side of her forehead.

She stopped playing but her hands hovered above the keys as if she wanted to continue but couldn't. Jay stood up and started walking. "You should stop doing this to yourself now Jay. It's been so long. You're hurting the people you love and..." He cut her in between.

"Why did you do that to me?" He turned around and she was still looking at the piano. "I loved you so much, and you did say the same to me. Then why?"

She laughed a little and stood up herself. "I love it when you forget that I'm not real, my love." Tears were in Jay's eyes again as she put her arms around his neck.

"Please come back." He started sobbing. "I need you so bad. I'm falling apart; now more than ever. I'll do anything. Just please come back to me."

She kissed his lips softly, to calm him down and wiped off his tears. "Never," she whispered close to his ear.

Jay Malhotra felt pity for himself.

He opened his eyes and she wasn't there; nor was he. It had happened a few hours ago when he had returned from Opera. Right now, he was on his way to his classroom looking as sober and normal as possible.

Jay entered the class and looked at the faces of his students, full of hope and excitement. In his frustration, Jay wanted to tell them that relationships don't go as perfectly they all think and love isn't as beautiful as he described. But he knew that whatever had happened to him was his own fault, not someone else's.

"Imagining; it's something that we all do every single day. Imagining about being with someone, imagining about hurting someone, imagining about going somewhere, imagining about anything and everything is our favorite part of our everyday routines. But sometimes, the idea of something is more beautiful than that actual thing. The idea of being in love, everyone is fascinated by it. The idea of being the love of someone special is something we all want. But perhaps we are in love with the idea of being with that person. Perhaps we love the idea of being in love with them. But we don't love them. It's harmful, a poison, you may say. It makes us happy but it isn't happiness. It's a lie that we tell ourselves and remain blind for as long as possible. Until the reality hurts us and shatters our feelings." He paused. "Just something for all of you to think about."

Chapter – 2

The Real Life Prince Charming

[Summer '07]

"Nice to meet you Amelia, your dress is really pretty," Jay said to me. That smile of his did not help stop me blushing. I wanted to reply but it was impossible to say anything to him.

"Hurry up man!" His cab driver yelled and sounded the horn. I'm a very polite person, but at that moment I wanted that driver to burn in hell. "I guess I'll see you around then." He shook my hand as he alighted from his cab. And all I could do was give a quick, shy wave as I saw him leave.

'You kissed his cheek. What on earth were you thinking Amelia?' I cursed myself as I walked back to my friends. I was not sure whether the last three minutes had been real and was not a dream. And it was even harder to believe that it was really him.

"Where did you go Amy?" Lily asked me as they stopped their playful gossip about the jerks they had a crush on.

"Nowhere," I replied quickly, as I did not want them to suspect anything. I was too shy to admit anything. It was hard enough not to smile… then the questions on top of that.

Jay was, I don't know, just something I did not want to get jinxed. They continued their conversation while I continued to think about my surreal moment.

I was sure something incredible would happen with me the moment I first entered the gates of SAU two weeks ago. Of course, it was just a fragment of my optimism but it came true. The instant I saw Jay, I fell in love with him. I know love at first sight is superficial and not something everyone believes in, but I did. After all, who doesn't believe something when it happens to them! He was everything I had ever imagined a man should be; handsome, talented, honest and so very sweet. Of course, I did not know much about him but I did know enough to understand that he'd be the man of my dreams.

The next day even when I wanted to, I couldn't stop thinking about him. My professor was lecturing about the greatest poets of all time; and I really wanted to concentrate on her words for I loved English. But that man would not leave my thoughts.The way he reacted shyly when I kissed his cheek and that smile, I get mini heart attacks every time I think about it.

"This concludes the poets of 19th century. Hope you all understood." Everyone said 'yes' in harmony. The professor looked at me for a second. "That's all for today."

Fortunately, the class got over without the professor realizing I hadn't listened to a single word she had said.

I got out of the class,all the while arranging my notes and again, cursing myself for being clumsy and inattentive, when I saw him again. The Jay Malhotra! Looking as perfect as he always did, going into a classroom for his English lecture. I don't know what, but there was something so irresistible about him that I always felt as attracted as a butterfly would to a beautiful flower.

His head was bent, looking down and he walked quietly into the classroom. He did not realize that a piece of paper had fallen from the notebook he was carrying. I rushed and picked up the paper before anyone else could.I was standing at the door of his classroom when I had the idea that I should sneak inside.It was so irrational that I did not pause to think how embarrassing it would be if anyone realized that I didn't belong there.

I sat on the last seat in a corner, so that the teacher couldn't see me. Luckily, the students didn't pay any attention to me either. I had lost Jay and in the crowd of so many faces. But thank God for his spark. As soon as I found him, I had that mini heart attack again. It's surprising how even a heart attack feels beautiful when in love.

I loved the way he sat there, silently, with just a smile, his pen constantly writing something. I literally did not have a care in the world. All there was for me was that person, sitting some faces afar.

"What are you writing Mr. Malhotra?" His professor asked him and I became nervous. I did not want anyone to say anything to him. "I have constantly said – no writing while I teach."

"Pardon me, professor. I did not mean to be disrespectful. It was important," Jay replied as he stood up.

"Would you like to share what was so important Mr. Malhotra?" She crossed her arms and now everyone was looking at him.

Jay was quiet for a minute as if he was thinking of something and then he spoke. "It's just that professor; I personally do not agree with you. There is a specific process of falling in, being in and falling out of love. That is what I was writing about."

"That is quite a theory Jay. And I personally do not agree with you. But it's a free country. Go on, I'd like to know what exactly you have for me."

Jay took a deep breath and presented his theory. "You are on top of a cliff; right on the brink. You look down and there that person is, the one who you want, waiting for you. You're not sure if they will catch you or not. But you jump; you take that leap of faith with your eyes closed. If you're lucky, they catch you in their arms safely and that is how you fall in love." He paused for a second.

If only I could tell him how mesmerizing he was. Every word out of his lips was like religion to me. I was at the top of that cliff and I had jumped to be with him. I knew he would be down there. I just wanted him to catch me. I didn't know why, but I knew that he would catch me. I trusted him.

In that excitement I clapped vigorously, loudly. "You go Jay!"

Everyone in the room turned to me with surprise and amusement. I had a wide smile on my face which started to fade, as I realized the embarrassment I was in. I did not realize that my hands continuedto clap, albeit slowly.

"I'm sorry, are you a student of this class?" Professor asked me.

I was frozen at my place, trying to come up with a legitimate answer. "Actually I, uh, I mean this is something…"

Suddenly my eyes met Jay's. He had a huge question mark on his face about me and that's when I came up with the best idea that came into my head at that time.

I ran as fast as I could out of the classroom with my bag. Everyone was looking after me, all confused,but entertained with my charming exit.I took a deep breath as soon I got out of the classroom. That was the most daring thing I had ever done. I could feel a little shortness of breath but I calmed myself down to not let it affect my day.

I sat outside in the gardens, working on my notes and eating a burger but still smiling, thinking about that man and his theories. Suddenly I realized I had Jay's piece of paper with me. I took it out and started reading.

I saw her yesterday, her white skirt flowing in air,

She was dancing with her friends, all beautiful and fair;

I couldn't take my eyes off of her stance, it looked

So very perfect, I tried to look away, but I was hooked.

She gave me happiness, she gave me hope,

She asked me to move fast if I wanted to cope

With her speed; alas her aura wore me

Out, but oh, I loved what I was seeing.

She was holding hands with the breeze,

Soaring high upon the clouds of dreams

And wishes; I wondered how was she

Still able to be so kind and so lovely,

She smiled at me and said, 'It's not easy

To be as me, but I let my roots define me

And let it decide where I should go."

There I was, standing speechless, "Whoa"

I said and looked at the marvelous sight

Of that magnificent and serene, kite.

"Mm; his words," I was mesmerized by his poem. It was so very beautiful. I took a big bite of my burger while thinking about that gorgeous boy.

"Hey Amelia," I looked up and Jay was standing there with a smile on his face.

I stood up quickly with surprise and my burger fell out of my hand. "Bhe bha bha," I replied or mostly coughed with my mouth full of food. It was more embarrassing than his expressions showed it to be.

"Huh? It's okay. You finish your bite first," he told me with a chuckle and caressed my back. He and I did not break our stare while I finished chewing what was in my mouth. My eyebrows were up with love and he looked at my clumsiness like it was the cutest thing in the world. "Is it better now?"

"Mmhm," I replied and laughed. "I'm sorry for that and also for what happened some time ago; in your class. I don't know what I was thinking." We sat on the bench together.

"Oh, that's okay. People love professor Duran and her teachings. So the curiosity from other students is genuine." If only he knew that my curiosity was to see him, and not the professor. "And, thank you for your applause," he laughed. "That was really sweet."

I felt shy at his words. It was embarrassing but if he found it sweet, then it wasn't a bad thing. "Would you like to tell me the whole 'process of love' that I interrupted earlier?" I asked him.

"I'd love to." He smiled and took out a notebook. It had a diagram with numberings and markings. "So, I already told you how you fall in love. Now the next step is to keep the relationship. You start walking on a road with the one you love, with your hand in theirs. But it's not that easy of course. The road is mesmerizing at first. Everything seems so very beautiful. But the more you walk, the worse the journey gets. It gets harder to keep smiling, harder to keep walking with their hand in yours. Then comes a point where they or you let go. If your bond is strong enough, then no one lets go and the journey ends with your death. But if you do let go, your journey of love endshalfway. That's when you slip to another route which takes you back to that cliff, again ready to fall in love. And you wait for someone to again, ask you to take that leap of faith." He looked at me. "That's how love works."

There was a moment of silence. I wanted to tell him how fascinating his words were and how much deeper I had fallen for him, but I couldn't say a single word. I just looked at him and he just looked at me. It was as if there was a rope around our bodies, pulling us towards each other. It was love.

"Hey, you beautiful man!" A guy appeared suddenly. I still did not pay attention to him. But, "Oh, hey Aarav. You're here." I could feel Jay getting a little nervous so I backed up a little, not letting his friend see our closeness.

"Yeah I am. Oh, I see you were busy Shriyut. Did I intrude?"

He called Jay Shriyut. That is when I looked at his friend and it stopped my heartbeat for a second.

"Oh no, it's okay. Amelia I'd like you to meet…Amy?!" Jay was stunned to see me collapsing.

"What the hell happened to her?" Aarav yelled as Jay caught me,as I fainted.

***

They sped to the hospital in Aarav's car. "Amelia? Amelia can you hear my voice?" Jay had her head in his lap as Aarav drove as fast as he could.

"Man, look at her phone, call her parents or someone," Aarav told Jay.

"Yeah okay." Jay took her phone out of her bag and called her mother's number.

"Amy, mom isn't here. What happened?" avoice at the other end said.

"Listen, I'm Amelia's friend. I don't know why,but she collapsed suddenly and we have just reached Sauveur Hospital. Please hurry!" Jay hung up the call in haste.

Aarav and he ran as fast as they could and hadher admitted. "We'll look after her, you please wait here." A nurse told them as she rushed down the emergency room with Amelia on the stretcher.

"It's all going to be okay, Shriyut. Don't worry." Aarav put his hand on Jay's shoulder and realized that he was bleeding. In the rush, Jay had cut his arm somewhere. "Dude your arm! Nurse, please have someone look at it."

"I'm fine Aarav. Don't worry," Jay told him but Aarav was persuasive.

"If you don't get stitched up, I'm going to tell Amy's family that it's your fault. She might tell them the truth later. But till that time, her father would've beaten the shit out of you," he said with a smug smile.

"Fine," Jay went into another room with the nurse.

A few minutes later, a girl approached the reception looking panicky. "I'm here for Amelia Prentiss."

"Hey, you're here for Amy. Don't worry she is going to be okay," Aarav told the girl. She resembled Amelia in a lot of ways; beautiful red hair and those enthralling eyes.

"Oh, thank you so very much. You don't know how much I appreciate that. I'm her sister, Elizabeth," she told Aarav.

"Nice to meet you. I'm Aarav and my friend is getting stitched up, Shriyut. He got cut a little," he replied.

"I hope he is okay. Please thank him as well." She shook Aarav's hand. Just then the doctor came up to them to tell them that Amelia was okay; just resting.

"Thank God. Can we please see her?" Elizabeth asked the doctor.

"She's asleep, but alright. Only family members though." the doctor replied.

Elizabeth thanked Aarav again and went in to see Amelia. Just then, Jay returned. "Oh Shriyut, you just missed Amy's sister. By the way, the doctor said that Amy's fine. But only family members can see her for now. I think we should go," Aarav told him.

"You don't know relieved I am," Jay collected his jacket from the table. "What did you say Amy's sister's name was?" he asked Aarav.

"She's Elizabeth; pretty girl."

"Oh, is that so? I'd love to meet her then," Jay replied with a laugh.

Chapter – 3

And He Did Catch Her, Right?

[The Present]

Jay was sitting in his classroom. It was a Sunday, but he did not care about that. He had a coffee cup on one side and a mountain of papers on the other. He had never liked coffee, but he needed it to sharpen up his mind. His mind was still obsessed with the happenings of the night before and of that morning.

Just then, Estella opened the door. She looked worried, and was searching for someone.

"Estella?" Jay called out and stood up.

She saw him and ran towards him with a smile. Jay was confused by herbehavior, and his confusion increased even more when she stopped close to him, breathing heavily. She hugged him tightly.

"Are you okay?" He asked her as he caressed her hair.

"Now I am," she whispered softly.

"Are you okay?" she asked him as she held his shoulder. She was standing beside him and he was still on his chair, wondering if he was hallucinating about the hug. But she really was there.

"Yes, I am," he replied, as soon as he realized the reality. "How did you find me Ms. Hudson?" he asked her, taking a sip of his coffee.

"I went to your apartment and the guard there told me you weren't home. So I checked here and the guard here told me that you're in."

"Could've just called me; anyways, how can I help you?"

She was searching for an answer. She had just wanted to talk to him about his past but she could see he wasn't ready. "Do you want some help sorting these papers out, Professor?" She asked him.

Jay had treated her with immense vindictiveness. He did want to make up to her. "They need to be in alphabetical order," he said, as he got her a chair to sit, and she smiled.

Estella kept looking at him every two minutes. He guessed that she wanted to start a conversation. "You can say whatever you want to Ms. Hudson. I don't bite."

She looked at him with surprise. "Are you sure?" she asked innocently.

Jay stopped working and gave her an embarrassed smile. "I'm sorry for last night. I accept that I am a rude person most of the time and I remind people of soul-eating ghosts. I'm fine with it. I don't really care about people's opinions; except my students', when I'm teaching." He paused. "But the way I was with you last night, I was a monster. And I know that's not who I am. I know that very well." He wanted to go on with his apology but she knew how guilty he felt.

"Professor, I understand," she said."Everyone has bad days. That was yours. Someday you might see mine." She smiled.

"It was a bad day. I wish it was just a day." He started his work again.

"I do understand," Estella replied. She wanted to say a lot to him but she was unable to form sentences.

"I know you do."

"What? What do you mean?" His words confused her.

"I meant, since your fiancée's death... Everyone has a different way of coping with sadness. I don't want to seem creepy but I have been seeing a figure outside my house every Thursday night. I got obsessed with whoever that was. And this week, I almost reached on time to talk to them. But I was a little late. I picked up a rose that was dropped there. Last night, your friends Laurel and Elizabeth told me that Agastya had died there so I figured it must be you."

Estella quietly continued to look at Jay. He could see her expressions changing; curiosity became frustration. "Yes," she replied. "It was me Professor Malhotra."

Jay could sense that she was uncomfortable but before he could apologize, she stood up. "Is everything okay, Estella?" he asked her as she collected her things in anger.

"Everything is perfectly okay professor. Everything is beyond perfect professor. Now if you will excuse me, I need to leave right this second." He had clearly hurt her. Jay was having a hard time believing his insensitivity; especially since he was trying to apologize to her for his behavior of the night before.

"I didn't...I didn't mean to hurt you," Jay thought to himself.

[Summer '07]

It had been a week that I had seen Amelia after her accident. I wanted to know if she was okay. I wished I had asked for her number or anything that would've kept me in contact with her. I sat on the same bench she had been sitting with me, while I had explained my 'process of love' to her. I was really worried for her and my anxiety made me restless. I did not realize that I was smiling unintentionally, thinking about the way she had been eating that burger that day.

I knew I needed to see her somehow. If only I wasn't one of those misunderstood people, it would've been easier.

I gathered my courage and knocked on the dean's office. "May I come in, ma'am?" She nodded yes without paying attention to who I was.

"How may I help you Mr. Malhotra?" she asked me, still not looking at me.

"You know my name," I said to her with a smile and then she saw my face.

"Not for the right reasons Jay," she replied disappointedly, referring to the incident that happened a couple of weeks ago.

"How did you know?" I was surprised and embarrassed.

"One of the students told me. Word gets around," she said to me, adding insult to injury.

I wanted to talk about it but I was there for another reason.

"Ma'am, I needed the contact number or address of Amelia Prentiss," I said in the most awkward tone. I knew she would think I just wanted to talk to Amelia and flirt with her.

She stared at me for a minute before she took off her glasses. "What is wrong with you?"

"Uh. What?"

"Mr. Malhotra, I'm explicitly telling you to stop being a punk and start concentrating on your studies again. The other day, I was told that you intentionally argued with Professor Sullivan about her theories.And now you are asking for a girl's number. What isgoingon with you? Do you want me to take away your scholarship? I can do that." Her anger spoke.

"No ma'am." I was never rude to my teachers and that moment was not going to be the first. "She is sick; really very sick. I just want to check on her, nothing else." I looked at her. I knew she believed me. "Please try to understand. I would never do anything to destroy your trust."

She continued to stare at me, wondering whether I was being honest. "Alright, Mr. Malhotra, but this would be the last time."

She gave me her home address and that was enough for me.

"Hey Aarav, I'm going to check on Amelia. I want to see if she is okay. Would you like to come with me?" I sent him a text. But instead of a reply, I got a call from him.

"You're going to see Amelia?" he asked me.

"Yeah, would you like to join me?"

He replied, 'Okaaaaaaay' and did not say anything for another ten seconds.

"So," he paused, "you would come late I think?"

"I think so. I'd have to change two trains to reach her place."

Another long 'okay' from him as a reply with a pause, "You go Shriyut; I have stuff to do."

I could sense that he was uncomfortable with my offer so I did not force him. I replied a long 'okay' and went on to attend my classes.

At 4 pm, I was at the subway, waiting for my train to take me to Amelia's. I had some time before the next train came, so I took out my notebook and tried to write something in it. I had always wanted to be a writer. My mother's dream for me was to see me at my first book's launch. My dream for myself was to see my parents at every big moment of my life. Of course, destiny had other plans. My mother became ill and then, that night happened.

I was on the verge of breaking down, when I saw a girl standing a little away from where I was sitting. Her long, dark hair was covering her face, troubling those red lips of hers, those lowered eyes of hers. I found myself getting lost; and that paradox is the reason I felt my heartbeat calm down. I was mentally listening to the most beautiful melody being played. I never thought I'd ever say this, but it felt as if I were in a movie.

I was facing her left side and she was facing the tracks. She turned her head around and I tried to see her eyes. They were perfect; so very perfect.I was getting sucked into those 'black holes' of hers. The gravity of her eyes was attracting me so much that I felt I was going to lose myself into them.

"Hey buddy, you don't want to catch your train?" a man sitting beside asked me.

"What? Oh yeah, the train is here," I looked at the girl, wanting for her to get on the train as well. But she did not move; so I did not either.

Three trains arrived and departed, neither of us cared about them. I did not remember why I was at that station, nor did I give much thought to why I was so concerned with her choices; all I knew was that she was there. And that's it.

Her crossed arms and frowning lips were enough to express the fact that she felt troubled. Perhaps she was waiting for someone, or she was not able to make up her mind. I got up and took a deep breath. I was going to talk to her. I wanted to comfort her and make her feel better. I did not care if I did not know her. I did not care what she might think. My intentions were clean and my heart was true.

Every step I took towards her was like a jolt of electricity. I was 20 feet away from her but reaching her took eternity. I was close to her – she smelled like the sunset. I wanted time to stop so that I could take her essence in.

"Excuse me," I said to her. She turned her head to me with a cold expression.

"Yes?"

I wanted to say what I was feeling… when I saw her eyes. I had seen those stunning blue eyes before. I wanted to tell her who I was, but I forgot how to speak. I stammered for a second before she got a call and left the station.

She must have thought that I was a freak.

After a lot of wasted time, I finally got on a train to reach Amelia's place. If only my head could stop thinking about that girl in the subway. But this was not the time to be romantic. I had to do what I was there to do. And not fool around.

I reached Amelia's at around 6:30 pm. She had a beautiful house. The walls were like unpainted bricks, but in a beautiful way. I was admiring the greenery and the architecture when a man came out of the house. I stopped him.

"Hey, I'm sorry to bother you. But is Amelia in? I'm a friend of hers."

"This is her house, yes but she is not here. She has been admitted in Santé Hospital, downtown. I'm her cousin. If you want, I can take you there."

"That'd be great. Thank you." We shook hands and sat in his car.

It took us thirty minutes to reach the hospital. "Come this way." Her cousin took me with him to Amelia and left, to look for her parents in the cafeteria. She was lying on the bed with headphones on. Her eyes were closed, so I did not go into the room. I stood looking at her from outside, wishing that she would feel better as soon as possible. She looked so beautiful.

"May I help you?" someone tapped me on the shoulder. I turned to see a doctor.

"Are you Amelia's doctor?" I asked him.

"Yes I am. Akshat Gupta." He shook my hand with a smile. He looked too young to be a doctor. I could comprehend he was about my age.

"Oh hello, I'm Jay Malhotra; Amelia's friend. I just wanted to know what happened to her. I was with her cousin who did not know anything either."

He looked at Amelia with sympathy in his eyes. "Jay, she has dilated cardiomyopathy. In simple words, her heart is swollen. It's mostly genetic and not an easy problem to diagnose. She has had this for a year now."

His words were heartbreaking. I had never thought that someone as remarkably wonderful as her would have to go through something like this. "What is the cure?" I asked the doctor.

"Heart transplant is the only option left for her. As a matter of fact, today she was supposed to get a new heart."

"So did she get it or will the transplant happen later?"

"Unfortunately it was given to someone who is in more need. It was her decision. She said she'd be happier to give it to whoever is in more need of it for she can survive without it for some more time; but that other patient cannot."

"People like her are rarely found on this planet. It's sad that she is going through so much," I told him, as my eyes got a little teary. "Can I see her please?"

"Sure."

I opened the door really gently and got into the room. She did not hear me come in. "Amy," I said softly.

She opened her eyes slowly and was shocked to see me there. "Jay!" she tried to get up but I quickly got her to continue lying down.

"Please do not get up. It's okay."

I sat beside her and held her hand. "How are you feeling?"

She gave me a beautiful smile. "I'm really good right now. But I was so surprised to see you. How are you here?"

"I just couldn't stop thinking about you. I needed to know how you were or else I would've gone crazy."

Her smile broadened. "Jay, you need to know something."

Her grip tightened a little.

"Go ahead."

"Okay." She took a deep breath. "The night you saved me, I was a little scared of you. I'm not used to violence. But as time passed, I started to fall for you. And I'll be honest – that day, when I was in your classroom, I was there to see you study. Every word you said that day has become imprinted in my heart." She laughed a little with shyness. "I am in love with you Jay. And I have fallen hard. All I wish is that someday you would feel the same." She could not even look at me – she was feeling very inhibited. She continued to look down at our hands and with a big smile.

"I already do, Amelia."

Her smile reduced and her eyes opened wide. "What?"

"I had such conflicting feelings before. Amy – I just did not know how to tell you about it." I tried to make her happy.

"Oh Jay. Oh my! I did not expect this." She was really very happy.

Her parents and her cousin entered the room. "Oh Amy! We did not know you had company. Look at that, our Amy is smiling after so long." I got up and introduced myself. I asked them to sit but they wanted to give us some space.

She held my hand again. "They are right. I haven't smiled for a long time. But today, I want you to know – this moment is like a dream come true for me Jay."

I kissed her forehead softly. "Get some sleep Amy." She agreed. We exchanged numbers and she closed her eyes. I got up to leave.

"You've made me the happiest girl on this planet Jay," she smiled.

"And I'm the happiest guy on earth." I couldn't look at her.

I had never had such conflicting feelings before. I was cursing myself for playing with the feelings of someone as wonderful as her; but at the same time, my optimism was telling me to be proud that I had made her smile. Throughout my ride home I was in a dilemma – should I tell her the truth or I should continue with my lie?

I took out my phone and sent her a text asking her not to tell anyone about it. It would just add to my guilt. 'Hey Amy, I hope you're feeling alright. It was really good to see you this evening. Just, please don't tell anyone about us yet. I'm not a people person. I hope you understand. Sleep well.'

'Oh, it's okay Jay. I completely understand. And, trust me; it was amazing to see you today. You made me feel better. Have a goodnight,' she replied. Her every word of love made me feel guiltier about everything.

I reached my apartment in a low frame of mind and an irritated face. I couldn't see anything – it was all too dark. I was still not familiar with the interior of the place but still tried to switch on the lights.

"SURPRISE!" I had a mini heart attack as I heard people yell, as soon as the lights came on.

There was a banner 'Welcome to Aarav-pad' above the heads of two dozen people, with ribbons and balloons everywhere. I had a little smile as I looked around. It was all Aarav's plan to make me feel welcome at his apartment. Then I understood why he had not joined me to meet Amelia.

I tried to thank everyone for the surprise, but their faces were in shock. "That's Jay Malhotra," a girl whispered loud enough for everyone to hear. I had not realized that I was Shriyut for Aarav before that moment.

I looked at him; he seemed broken and angry at the same time. And then suddenly, the commotion started. Everyone started talking about that night and the fact that I was not Shriyut, as Aarav had told them.

I was scared. There was nothing left for me to tell Aarav at that moment. I knew that those present would execute me with embarrassment. In panic, I rushed to my room and closed the door behind me.

Chapter – 4

Seeing is Believing

[Summer '07]

(Three Weeks Ago)

"Guys, my-my head is spinning," Aarav said to his friends.

"Doesn't matter man; you still have to do it," Kyle told him, as he gulped down another can of beer.

"Ky-Kyle, I-I-I have had six cans-cans already. I-I shouldn't," he stammered drunkenly.

"You are not allowed to back out you-you piece of chicken! Are you a homo chicken, Aarav?"

"Yeah Aarav, are you a chicken?" Peer pressure was building up on Aarav and he gave in to it.

"I'm not a chicken! I'll do it." Everyone yelled in joy and hooted for Aarav as he took a mouthful of beer.

Meanwhile, a group of new students were celebrating their admission into SAU.

"Cheers to two years of amazing life and a bright future ahead," Lily toasted and the girls raised their glasses.

Amelia had already told everyone about her condition and they respected her decision to drink just an iced tea.

Aarav reached the group of girls with a drunken face and wobbly walk. "Freshmen?" he asked the girls.

The girls had judged that Aarav's intentions were not nice. "We don't want any trouble, sir," Lily said to him.

"Trouble?" he laughed manically. "Want to party?" He came close to the group and the girls became scared. Aarav's friends were a little far away, sitting in Kyle's SUV, laughing and watching carefully.

"Please get away sir," a frightened Amelia requested Aarav.

"Hey, j-just want to party." He was about to hold Amelia's hand when someone shoved him aside firmly and slapped him. He fell to the ground.

"What the…" Before Aarav could say something else, he was slapped again.

"Get the hell away from the girls or I'm calling the cops," the man said.

Aarav's friends got into the cars and drove away instantly. Before Aarav could threaten the man for hitting him, he realized how insulting the situation was getting for him. Everyone was staring at himas if he were trying to assault the girls, which in a way, he was. So he decided that it was better to run for now than to get slapped again.

"I'll remember this," Aarav whispered as he left.

The man turned to the girls. "Is everyone alright?" By that time, people had recognized the man to be Jay.

"Yes, we are. Are you okay?" Alexis asked him.

"And thank you so much for that,"she said a little awkwardly. "It was scary."

Unfortunately, people around them did not knowthat Jay was a Good Samaritan. It's natural for people to make assumptions in their mind about a particular situation. And they did. Everyone who had watched the men fight thought of Jay as the bully and Aarav as the victim.

"It's alright. I think I should go. You all take care." His eyes met Amelia's for the first time.She seemed a little afraid of Jay's actions.

Everyone in the University came tothe conclusion that Jay Malhotra was a bully. Most people did not know anything about him other than his name. But this was enough to degrade him. Stories began to float around about his 'previous' bullying acts.

"I heard that he was kicked out of his high school because he beat a guy to death."

"Yeah, I have heard that too. I'm sure Jay wanted to kill Aarav Mehta the other day just because he was asking out the girl whom he liked." Two friends gossiped as if they knew everything about Jay's life. No one actually knew who Jay Malhotra was or what he looked like. He existed, that was enough for them to spin yarns of about him.

Aarav was probably the only person in the world whose life got better after trying to commit an offensive act. Everyone sympathized with him, calling him brave, telling him, "We admire you. You're so non-violent Aarav." He did not disagree with anyone, but kept thanking them for theircompliments. However, deep down Aarav knew that something wasn't right.

"Hey Kyle, what exactly happened last night? Who is this Jay Malhotra? Why did he beat me?" Aarav cornered Kyle, trying to get a clear picture about what had transpired.

"Hey look man, it was just a misunderstanding. You were drunk and before we could say anything, you approached some freshmen and flirted with them. That Jay guy thought that you were trying to molest the girls. So he beat you up. It was his entire fault and a little was yours too. We had nothing to do with it." Kyle suddenly had Aarav's whole group behind him.Everyone was trying to tell Aarav the same story, a little differently. But no one seemed confident. They were all trying to keep themselves out of the story, which was a wake-up call for Aarav. He decided to distance himself from these people.

It had been three days since that night. No one had tried to understand Jay's point of view.He did not care to clarify it either. Very few people knew who he was and they believed that he could not have been the bad guy in the situation. But before they could say anything to anyone, Jay requested them not to argue with anyone regarding anything and let everyone think what they wanted to.

"But Jay, almost the whole university is talking all kinds of crap about you. Why don't you reveal the truth?" Ellie asked him.

"I do not care what anyone thinks. If I did I would already have painted my chest with the words 'I'm not a bad person.' I am not here to win the elections or be a movie star. I care about my studies. That's all" Jay replied softly, as he did not want anyone to overhear his words to Ellie in the café.

"Next please!" the barista called.

"Yeah, I will have a regular Choco Macchiato and he will have an iced tea," Ellie ordered.

"Names please?"

"Ellie and..." Jay was about to say his name when he realized how popular he was in the university at that moment!

"And he is Shriyut," Ellie replied quickly, before Jay could say anything.

"What are you doing?" Jay asked her.

"This is the best way to keep you hidden until this whole situation blows over. You might think it's crazy or childish but this is a social life. You cannot understand it better than I do, so shush." Ellie tried to convince Jay. But she was right; he thought it was crazy and unnecessary.

It was raining when Jay got out of the café. He saw a frantic man in an expensive-looking suit, panicking. He did not even care that he was getting wet from the rain. It was obvious that the man was searching for something.

"Is everything okay, sir?" Jaystepped into the rain and asked him.

That man suddenly sported a smile on his face. "You're such a sweet young man. Yes, actually you can help me. My son has been in some kind of a difficult situation with some other kid and I'm trying to find him. Could you please tell me where to go?" he replied, as he tried to cover his bald head with his handkerchief. Jay felt really bad for the man.

"I don't know if I could do that but you know what, why don't you come with me into this café first? We need to get you out of the rain and give you something warm to drink." The man accepted Jay's offer with a big smile.They ran inside the café.

While they were stepping inside, Jay bumped into a girl dancing with little kids. She fell and took Jay's bag down with her.

"Oh I'm so sorry," he helped her get up and started collecting his notes. He could not see her face because her hair was all over her face. But he did see her royal blue eyes. Jay wanted to say something to her. He wanted to tell her how stunning she was, but words forgot to come out of his mouth. Before he realized she was back to the kids, playing with them.

"Come in, son. The weather is getting really bad." The man called Jay, breaking his hypnotized state and he stepped in. But the girl's eyes were fixed in his mind.

"So, who's your son?" Jay got his new friend a cup of tea, and lemon tea for himself as they sat down in a corner.

"Oh, he's Aarav Mehta." As soon as Jay heard Aarav's name, he wanted to run away. He was already in a lot of problems because of him – only God knew what would happen if his father recognized that he was the person his son had had the fight with."He is doing his MBA from here. Unfortunately, I have not visitedthis university before, so I did not know where the departments are. I am Arnav Mehta, by the way," Mr. Mehta told Jay, with his signature smile. "I'm so sorry son; I didn't even ask you your name."

Jay was trying to think what the appropriate reply to Arnav's question would be, when it hit him. "I'm Shriyut." It was Jay who was getting hysterical then.

"That's a unique name. Seems a little made-up," Arnav laughed and Jay joined in with a fake one. "So what are you doing here?"

"I am a student of Psychology sir," Jay added another aspect to his new character.

"Oh, that's fascinating. I would want you to read my face and tell me something about myself," he said with another laugh. Jay realized that Aarav's father was not taking him seriously. So he decided to make him take him seriously.

"Sir, anyone with a good sense of human emotions can read faces, I'll do you one better. I'll tell you what you don't show on your face." Arnav could be seen losing his smile a little. "You love your son, but this is not the first time he has been in a 'difficult situation' with someone. And you're really nervous about what the authorities or other students would have to say about it. You are an honest man –your have worked hard all your life. You believe in family like it's shown in Italian mafia movies. Your life's work, success, and buildup, everything is just for your family. Your son is very important you. You have invested a lot of your health and knowledge to make him a beautiful human being. Unfortunately, he is stumbling a little, struggling to be who he is supposed to be. But you won't let him fall. You will save him. Am I not right?"

There was a spark in Arnav's eyes. He was so hypnotized by Jay's words, that he did not pay any attention to the fact that Jay had only stated the probable facts that would seem true in relation to his situation.

"You're a slice of magic my son." He held Jay's hand. "I wish my son had a friend like you. Your parents must be really proud of you," he said with a smile.

"They passed away in a car accident when I was little sir," Jay stated, losing his smile.

"I'm sorry to hear that. Don't worry, wherever they are, they're proud." He paused for a second. "Where do you live?"

"I live off campus. I have a room there," Jay replied,showing disappointment. His present living conditions were not at all comfortable for him and the topic of moving had been on his mind for weeks.

Arnav suddenly had a flash of inspiration and took out his card. "This is my number, call me by tomorrow. My son lives alone in his lavish apartment and I'd really want someone like you to live with him." Jay wanted to politely refuse his offer. "Please, just think about it."

"I will call you sir. Thank you so much." There was no harm in taking a look at the place. His current place was really small and was getting uncomfortable.

Jay and Arnav hugged each other and said their goodbyes. It was surreal for both of them – to meet someone so nice out of nowhere. Arnav told his son all about the magical person he had met – which made Aarav jealous. He was not thoughtful enough to understandthat his father cared for him very much,and that his recent behavior had disappointed him.

That night, when Jay got home, his mind was ready to burst with the thoughts of the girl. So he took out his diary and wrote something down.

It was pouring rain in the month of July,

I was damp and dirty and cursed the sky,

I saw a girl, dancing towards me with gaiety,

She bumped into me while revolving happily,

I collected my work, wanting to shout something,

Butmy heart stopped beating, soul started to sing,

Her stunning eyes, were sapphirein color,

I held her hand and forgot my anger,

Her electric touch was like the heavens,

Her stare took my heartbeat to a new level,

My mouth stopped working and so did my mind,

She then continued her dance, and I had a smile.

***

"He said, 'I want you to show him your apartment and get him to live with you. He's a really a good guy and far better than all your friends.' I remember him specifically saying that." Aarav was talking to himself. "This man is my father's choice; a person who proves me weak in front of the whole university and then lies about his identity to live with me."

No party had happened. Everyone had left as soon as they sensed the tension between Jay and Aarav. However, the place looked worse than the aftermath scene of a party. The decorations had been torn apart, tables were upside down with food and liquor spilled all over the room.

"Stop it Aarav," Jay pushed open the door to Aarav's room and entered. "I told you, I'm sorry for lying to you and your father. I got nervous and it just sort of happened."

But Aarav was not at all ready to listen to anything. "Get the hell out of my room and not just here… I want you gone from this apartment instantly. I don't want to live with a liar."He pushed Jay out of his room.

Jay regained his balance and stood there looking at Aarav. "You want me gone? I'll go. But you need to know the truth. I hid my identity from you to save you from embarrassment.

Yes, you. I don't know how you never thought of apologizing to the girls whom you had mistreated that night when you were blind drunk." Aarav's expressions started to change. "I never cared about what people think about me, but I really care about what you think about me; because I care about you. For the first time I felt I had a brother, a family member. I could've told you the truth. I could've told you that the reason I slapped you that night was because you were out of line and insanely inappropriate. Anyone would've done the same. But you know the worst part? This world made me the one in the wrong. And that's gotten inside your mind. You were the one who was wrong that night. I merely tried to save the ladies. I didn't deserve the words I have been called. Sure, it doesn't matter to me. But it still hurts." He straightened his shirt. "I'll leave by morning. Don't worry. Thank you for everything though. I'll remember that."

He walked towards his room. "Oh and I'm sorry for lying." Jay closed the door of his room behind him.

When Aarav woke up, the whole apartment was beautifully clean. Jay had spent most of the night cleaning the place up. Aarav looked to his right – Jay was all packed to leave. It hadn't taken him long, since he had not unpacked his belongings fully and set them up as yet.

Aarav went to the kitchen counter and poured cornflakes into a bowl. He looked at Jay as he was throwing out the trash, not saying a single word.

"Leaving?" Aarav asked Jay.

They stared at each other for a second. "Yeah, just you know. Cleaning a little; I don't like to leave a place dirty," Jay replied.

Jay was wishing that Aarav to say something, but Aarav did not seem to be interested in stopping Jay from leaving. It did not take Jay long to understand that.

"Okay then," Jay picked up his bags. "Bye Aarav."

"Oh, come on man!" Aarav yelled. "You can't make me so emotional dude. That's against the rules."

"What rules?"

"The rules which state that Aarav will apologize to Jay for being such a moron and ask him if he would like to you know, not leave," Aarav took Jay's bags from him.

Jay hugged him with a smile. "Apology accepted. And I'm sorry too, for lying. I never meant to hurt you."

"It's all good Shriyut," Aarav replied with a smile.

Jay laughed, "It's Jay. Jay Malhotra."

"Right, Jay. I always had a doubt that Shriyut was a made-up name." Aarav pulled Jay's cheek with a grin. "So your name is Jay. And can I also call you J?" He pointed his index fingers at Jay waiting for him to get the joke.

"What on earth did you just say? I didn't understand anything."

Aarav's grin was gone. "Never mind; I read it in some novel. It was pretty good actually." Aarav narrated the plot of the novel as they walked towards the kitchen and Jay started to cook breakfast.

Chapter – 5

The Fallen Angel

[The Present]

Estella entered the Opera's doors after a long time. It always reminded her the first time she had met Agastya. The way he sang, the way he had looked, the way he had flirted, the way he made fun of himself and the way he had swept Estella off of her feet – it was all clear to her as if it had happened the day before.

But at that moment, she was angrier at Jay than she was missing Agastya. He had no right to interfere with her life. She could do anything in any way she wanted and he should stay out of her judgments and decisions. Besides, how could Laurel and Kathryn tell Jay about Agastya? He wasn't their fiancé. They were not the one reeling from the loss of the one they truly loved. Estella was.

"What can I get you?" the bartender asked her.

"Just get me something strong. I don't care what it is," Estella replied coldly.

"Can you tell me something specific ma'am?" he asked and Estella shot him a look that scared him. "Just asking, lady! No need to get all weird."

"She'll have whiskey," the girl beside Estella replied.

The bartender thanked the other girl and got Estella a whiskey. It did not take long for Estella to realize that she was being inappropriate. "I'm sorry for being a psycho. I didn't mean to be." She apologized to the other girl.

"That's okay." She smiled. "It happens to the best of us. Trust me; I know what I'm talking about." The girl took a big sip of her drink.

Estella felt she was nice. "I'm Estella."

"I'm Elizabeth. You can call me Liz," Elizabeth replied and shook her hand. "Hey, you've written the annual plays at SAU, right?"

Estella gave an awkward laugh. "I didn't know it was so official."

"Oh no, Aarav told me. He and I are good friends. He talks about you a lot; nice to see you in person."

It did not take Estella a second to realize that Liz was Amelia's sister. How many other girls with red hair were named Elizabeth in the city? It was a long shot but Estella felt confident she was right.

"Oh, your sister Amelia was a student of SAU, right? I've heard she was really beautiful. I'm sorry to hear about what happened to her." Estella did not want Elizabeth to guess that she knew what happened between her sister and Jay.

"Yes, she was stunning. Even when she got really sick, she had a glow on her face that was enough to make her one of most beautiful people on earth." Elizabeth smiled thinking about her sister. But very slowly that smile started to fade. Elizabeth was thinking about the other night, when she had confronted Jay about his debauchery. Of course, she knew deep down in her heart that Jay would never have tried to hurt Amelia. But a niggling doubt remained.

"Tell me about her." Estella said. Her smile was something everyone felt hypnotized by. At that point of time, Estella looked like a storm in the sea and her smile was similar to a little ship, trying it's best to stay afloat and not get destroyed. There was a contradiction, an ambiguity that just enhanced her magnificence.

Elizabeth too, could not stop herself from being hypnotized by it. "Alright Estella," she replied. "I'll tell you about Amy." And she began by relating childhood memories of her and her sister. Estella could see the spark in her eyes, while she spoke about Amelia. Estella finally realized that she had suffered a similar loss. And that made her listen to Elizabeth with even more interest.

[Summer '07]

"There she is, my beautiful Amelia!" Elizabeth entered the hospital room and jumped on the bed. I hugged her as tightly as I could. We greet each other this way every time she came to visit me. It was a ritual being we had followed since the first time I had been admitted in hospital because of my condition.

"You know, I think I permanently need to stay here. My eyes seem more beautiful," I joked.But Elizabeth being the best sister she was, did not appreciate it.

I could see her losing her smile. She stared at me for a second. "Amy, please don't say that. Do you know how much I pray day and night for you to get better as soon as possible?" She had a little tear that was trying to squeeze itself out of her eye.

"Oh my cute little baby, I'm so sorry." I wiped her tear. Sometimes I go overboard with my 'humor' regarding my condition – so I tried to cheer her up. "You want to know something amazing!" I said excitedly, with a huge smile. I had been waiting to tell my sister about Jay. Oh, it was still so hard for me to believe that he, and I quote, had 'strong feelings' for me. The last couple of hours had been surreal for me. And the best person to be the first to hear about it would be my sister.

"Yes, yes!" She smiled finally. "Tell me."

"Okay so, the thing is that…" Before I could say anything to her, I got a text from Jay, asking me not to say anything to anyone. I found it really cute that he was such a shy being. He also texted that he loved meeting me and my damaged heart skipped beats.

"Are you going to say anything? Whose text is it?" Elizabeth asked me.

I replied to Jay's text and did not know what to tell my sister. "It's just a classmate asking how I am; nobody important." I tried to hide it from her. But she knew every little expression of mine. It did not take her much to catch my lie.

"Oh hush, you liar! Tell me the truth – who was it?" She attempted to snatch my phone from me.Then we both spent a minute wrestling over my phone. "Tell me the truth dammit or I'll break your phone with no regrets!"

"Alright, alright; calm down. I'll tell you." I gave in to her wish eventually. "Okay look, for some time I liked this guy really very much. He's sweet, cute, he's passionate about his workand he's caring…" I took a deep breath "He's perfect Liz. And I'm in love with him." Elizabeth was busy admiring my smile. It was a smile that she had not seen on my facebefore.

And I understood her reaction, I had never been so smitten by anyone ever before.

"Oh my God, Amy; that's so amazing! Who is he and when did this happen?" She was really excited, wanting to know who it was, but thanks to Jay's text I could not tell her.

"He's…" I paused, wondering what to reply. I so wanted her to know the truth. I wanted her to meet 'my man', but I had to respect Jay's wishes. "He's Moi Seigneur," I replied with a secretivesmile.

"Moi Seigneur is French for 'My God'." She gave a smug smile. "Oh my God Amy." She said and we both laughed.

"Stop it. He's just not yet ready to tell everyone about it. We just confessed our feelings for each other today. We can't go all public so soon," I told her as she and I layon my hospital bed.

She held me from behind. "I'm so happy for you Amy. I just hope you find the happiness you deserve; the purest kind."

It was my turn to have tears in my eyes. I had been really scared of dying and the main reason being my sister. She was as precious to me as anything can be. She had been my rock in all those times of fear, sadness and pain. It was really exciting to know that she finally had someone to share that burden with and I couldn't wait for him to finally be ready to meet her.

I kissed her hand and asked her to go to sleep but I realized she already was. I was really proud to see my sister being so responsible and mature. It was hard to believe that she was the same person who had been so scared of Barney the dinosaur.

I really wanted Jay to visit me sooner but my sister just wouldn't leave. She was trying her best to meet him and to know more about him. I even told my parents not to say anything about Jay to her and they agreed.

It wasn't like I hated her presence. It was really heartwarming to know that she cared about me so much. Besides, Jay and I had been texting each other constantly. He would tell me how beautiful I was and how much I meant to him. The first message he sent to start the conversation was to ask me was how I was feeling and I would reply how his text had made me feel better. I was not sure if it was all a dream or that my life really was a fairy tale. The perfect guy was mine, and cared about me more than anything.

"He's just so dreamy Liz. I can't wrap my head around the fact that perfection does exist in this world." It would be my most frequent reply to Elizabeth whenever she asked me about him, taking a deep, romantic breath.

"When am I going to meet your 'Seigneur' Amy? Or should I directly go to a church or a temple to see him?" She would tease me once in a while. Well, only when I was not talking about him, which was very rare.

Then one evening, I got a text. 'Hey Amy, how're you feeling now?' It was Jay.

His every text had the same effect on my injured heart. It would start dancing like nothing had happened. 'I was okay, but right now I'm much better.' I replied and a smile automatically appeared on my face.

'Oh, great;would it be possible for me to come over? I really want to see you.'

Yes, I really was dancing at that point. It was such a perfect moment because Liz had gone back to the house to arrange things for my return, when I got discharged from the hospital.

And there was no one to make Jay uncomfortable about our relationship.

'Of course, you can. I'm going nowhere yet. I really want to see you too.' I jumped out of the bed and rushed into the restroom to look my best for him. It was the second time he was visiting me in the last one week. He had met me once last week too, but it had been too brief for us to talk properly. I brushed my hair and practiced my smile. I was looking horrible courtesy of my medicines but I hoped he would say that I looked nice.

I got back on the bed when I heard a knock on the door. "It's Jay, may I come in Amy?"

I took a deep breath to calm myself down. "Yes of course, come in!" He looked as amazing as he always did and all I wanted was for him to take me in his arms and run away.

"I forgot to tell you. I got a call from Aarav, your friend. He apologized to me for his drunken actions that night and requested me to convey apologies from him to every one of my friends. I think that's really sweet of him.

He stared at me for a second. "You look so beautiful." He sat down on the edge of my bed. He couldn't see how my soul was completing its checklist for its mate. And had chosen his; as the perfect candidate.

I was done being shy. I had to tell him how crazy he continued to make me in his love. "I told my sister about you. Don't worry, I didn't tell her who you are or your name. I just told her I'm in love with someone and that the person is 'Moi Seigneur' – it means my Divinity or God. And that's what you are to me. You're that spirit we read about in stories who comes along every generation to make everyone happy.

All I'm trying to tell you is how much you mean to me." I held his hand firmly and smiled. But, he was not smiling. Nor was he looking at me.

"I don't love you Amelia."

"What?"

"I lied about my feelings for you. I just wanted you to feel better. I did not mean to hurt you in any way but I just can't keep pretending that I'm in love with you. I think you're an amazing girl and to be honest, out of my league. But I do not have strong feelings for you. I thought I could continue with it and someday I really might start to love you but I can't pretend anymore. Not right now when I know that there is someone else I'm falling for. Hate me Amelia. I lied." He still did not look at me.

He said he was falling for someone. And she wasn't me.

"Hey, it's okay. I understand you just wanted me to be happy and get better soon. I'm sorry I'm so clingy though. It wouldn't have happened if I were not so open about my feelings for you. Trust me, it's all okay." He still was not looking at me. "To be honest I realized that you were just a crush too. Don't worry, in some time it'll be over and things will get back to normal."

"I do care about you."

I was trying to think of a reply. "You should go now. My parents and sister will be here soon and I don't want any drama." We both were quiet for half a minute. And then he got up to leave.

I did not let him know how shattered I was from inside. I wanted him to leave as soon as possible so I could finally stop pretending to be okay.

"I'm sorry," he said.

"It's always okay," I lied.

As soon as he left, I ran into the bathroom and cried my eyes out. He had broken my heart and even though he did not mean to, he did hurt me. He hurt me so bad that I couldn't even breathe properly. Then I realized, I was having one of my panic attacks again and before I could shout for help, I was down on the ground, unconscious.

***

Jay got out of the hospital and it started to rain heavily. Before he could step out in the rain, he got a call.

"Meet me near the cattle ranch," the voice said.

"Is it something urgent? It's raining," he asked.

"I won't repeat myself. Come there as soon as possible."

Before Jay could say anything else, the person at the other end hung up. He wanted to go back inside and talk to Amelia again, but he couldn't have. He was too embarrassed to. So he decided to go to the cattle ranch.

"Aarav, I'm texting you Amelia's hospital address and room number. Just go and meet her once. She'll feel better.

"Did you do it?"

"Yes," Jay replied. "I broke her heart."

Chapter – 6

The Instrument of Harmony

[Summer '07]

(Two Weeks Ago)

I always believed in the power of universe. I strongly held this philosophy that we are all meant to follow a path.Every choice we make takes us forward on it. If we change who we are and take different decisions in the hope that we will be able to change our destiny, then we're wrong. Because the changed, new path was the one we were supposed to be on since the start. No matter how hard we try, no matter how much we struggle, we cannot outrun our destiny.

I knew I was ruining Amelia's life since the moment I told her I felt the same for her as she did for me. I tried to tell myself that I did the right thing; I even tried to make myself believe that my subconscious did have feelings for her. But who was I kidding? I knew she was just someone who gave me a warm feeling in my heart. That did not mean I was in love with her.

"Aarav, I did a terrible thing." I went inside Aarav's classroom where he was working on his notes and told him the truth about everything that had happened. I needed to let it out to someone or I would've gone crazy. "Amelia is suffering from cardiomyopathy. It's a heart condition that can be fatal. I went to see her the other day and before I could say anything, she told me that she was in love with me. I did not want to break her heart, so I panicked and told her I felt the same. So basically, she now thinks we're in a relationship."

Aarav was distraught."Jay, man, you shouldn't have done that. That's horrible. You can't play with someone, especially a girl who is in love with you." I expected him to say something like that. He was right, I couldn't have done that to her. But I just wanted her happy. I just wanted her to feel as better as soon as possible. She was special, she was amazing. But I was like an addiction to her. She thought that I was making her feel good, but the truth was that I was hurting her without her knowledge.

I was so engrossed in my thoughts that I did not realize that Aarav was still lecturing me. I had had enough. I did not want to hear anything about it so I stood up.

"I need fresh air," I cut him in between his preaching.

"Jay," he stopped me. "You need to end this, soon."I did not look at him and just left. He was right, but I wish I knew how to do that.

I switched my mind off and walked on the straight path to Reindeer Gardens. The serene sound of the trees swaying gave me peace. But of course, my mind was still fixed on my guilt. I was trying to distract myself but of course, that is never easy to do when you're bewildered and there is no answer to any of your questions.

I sat down on bench overlooking the lake,with the petals of cherry blossom falling down it softly. That's how death is supposed to be. Like being the petal of a cherry blossom tree and falling into a lake with tranquility and composure.

I looked on my right and saw someone swinging in the children's empty playgroundat a little distance. Only, she was not a child. She had her sandals in her hands and was making a cute sound – 'wee' – every time she swung forward. Her stunning hair was covering her face and I tried hard to see who she was, but I couldn't.

I did not realize when exactly I started smiling. All my thoughts were concentrating on the enigma of that girl. Nor did I realize when I had started walking towards her. A deep, religious part of me believed that I knew her or perhaps I was supposed to know her.

I unknowingly, unintentionally walked close to her. And she stopped swinging suddenly. She stood up, still holding her sandals in her hands. She turned back to me as the little breeze made her hair wave in the air, as the sun shone in the background. It was again, like a scene out of a movie. I should've been surprised to see who she was, but I had a little hunch that she was indeed the girl from the subway, as soon as I saw her on the swing.

"Are you stalking me – outside the café, the subway the other day, then here today?" she asked me with a frown.

"I'm sorry; I didn't know someone else would be here. The garden is closed at this time of the afternoon," I told her.

"It is, but the gatekeeper knows my father. He lets me in whenever I want," she replied.

"Mr. Gaurav. Yes, he's a nice person," I could feel my heart pounding in my mouth. "I'll leave you alone."

"You're Jay Malhotra, aren't you; the person who beat up a guy a couple of weeks ago?" She sat down on the swing and gestured to me to sit beside her. I had never been a very open person, or an extrovert. But I sat on the swing next to her when she told me to.

"Yes." I did not like that everyone judged who I was on the basis of that night. But honestly, I never cared about who thought what of me. However, I wanted to seem a better person to her.

"I was there when you were going all Bruce Lee on that guy, Aarav Mehta," she said. "Although I know you were not wrong in your place. He did misbehave."

"You're the first person I have come across other than the girls he misbehaved with, to take my side." She started to swing slowly. "Aarav is a great guy. Everyone make mistakes – this was his."

"I'm sure," she said. "What were you going to say to me on the subway?"

Her question honestly made me freeze again. I had no answer to it without seeming creepy. I wanted to tell her that she looked pretty but I choked in nervousness. "I was just going to ask the time," I said. I knew she understood that I was lying, but it was better than saying something unpleasant to make her uncomfortable. "Why did you take off your sandals?"

She looked at me then at her feet. "I like the way grass feels." She put her feet in the grass and softly rubbed it. Then she got off the swing and started walking, and I joined her.

"What's your name?" I asked as she stood by the lake admiring the cherry blossom trees where I had been sitting before.

She looked at me and gave a smile. "Why?" she asked me.

"I want to know what to call you."

"Why would you call me anything?"

I paused to thinkof a reply. "I don't know." I could clearly see that she was not interested in talking to me.

She smiled at my awkwardness. "Viola Harris."

I was in a trance. While searching for something else, I had found her. What serendipity!"It's nice to meet you Viola Harris." I smiled and accidently my notebook fell out of my coat.

"What is this?" She snatched it from the ground quickly before I could pick it up and I again started to panic.

"Oh that's not something I show people. Give it back to me." I tried to take it from her but she was not interested in giving it to me.

"You've written poems here." She turned the pages with a chuckle but then she stopped. "It says this one is for the subway girl." She gave it back to me. "Is it for me Jay Malhotra?" she asked me.

I sat down on the bench and stared down. I did not know how she would react if I said yes.

She walked and stood really close to me.Her head was inches away from mine. I could smell the aroma of her hair on my face. "Look at me, Jay Malhotra. Look into my eyes," she whispered to me. I was flustered but I did as she told me to. "Don't be embarrassed of something you feel proud of doing; ever." I unintentionally nodded. "So I ask you again. Is this poem for me?"

"Yes," I replied and her head was still close to mine. I could hear my heartbeat so loudly as if I had a stethoscope in my ears.

"Okay," she said and sat beside me."Just for the record, I still think it's a little creepy," she smiled.

I was sitting alone in the dark,

When I linked the night to an arc

And I found myself surrounded;

Lost, mesmerized and confounded

With the thoughts of your eyes,

If only my words could suffice

What that one look does to me,

And how so suddenly I feel free

Of all the worlds' rage and gloom;

Your eyes make my heart bloom,

Like a little flower in the meadow,

Or the setting sun casting a shadow;

It is funny how something so shy

Can make your entire soul cry

For its beauty lies in the antiquity

Of its perfection being, oh so gritty!

I don't think she was expecting it to be good at all, but she found it better than she thought it would be.

"I-this... okay," she was trying to think of what to say. And then suddenly, she kissed my cheek softly. "This was really very beautiful. I'm honored to know that you wrote this for me."

I was at the height of my shyness. I was feeling the way the petals of that cherry blossom tree were feeling. The only difference was they did not symbolize death anymore, they symbolized something else. What exactly was it? The feeling you get when you look at someone smiling and realize that you're the reason. You want to get closer to them but are afraid of that intensity, that passion. So you are stuck in between. It's not love; it's not just a crush. It's something in between and it is the most confusing thing in the world.

"I'll remember this day," she stood up. And so did I. "I have to go."

I wanted to urge her to stay for a little while longer but I did not want to ruin the impression I had made on her. "Thank you Viola."

"But, for what?" She laughed.

"Long story."

"I'm a student of biotechnology; final year. Come see me in the south campus if you ever want to. I'll be waiting," she said with a smile. "Bye, Jay Malhotra."

"Bye, Viola Harris."

Destiny; cannot run away from it. Perhaps it was in mine to meet her. Maybe that was the start to something. I could never be sure of anything but somehow I did not doubt it either. Even when I was trying, I was not able to wipe her face or her fascinating smile out of my mind.

It was exhilarating.

I went directly to my apartment to tell Aarav all about what had happened but as I was entering the building, thoughts of

Amelia came back to me. So I changed my mind and left to see her at the hospital. I directly went inside without caring about who was there and who wasn't.

"May I come in Amy?" I asked her, knocking on her door.

"Jay! You're here! Oh crap, I; wait, I'm sorry. Come in please," she replied in excitement and I entered.

"How're you feeling now Amelia?" I asked her.

"I was okay but now I'm feeling much better," she always replied with the same word to that question.

I gave a smile. I wanted to tell her the truth and I thought it would be the best time to say it. "So listen, I needed to talk to you about something." Before I could say something, her parents entered the room.

"Oh hello Jay, we did not know you were here," Mr. Prentiss greeted me.

"See, I told you there is something going on between them," Amelia's mother said to her father.

"Just because he has come to meet her, that does not mean they're dating babe," he replied.

"Yes, it doesn't. But look at Amy. Her face gives it away. She is so much in love with him."

"Mom, stop!" Amy yelled. She was trying to keep her promise of not letting anyone know about our relationship. But she looked at me and I understood what she wanted to say. Her eyes were trying to ask my permission to tell her parents the truth.

And my smile gave her the permission.

Her parents were really happy with the news but she made them promise that they wouldn't say anything to Elizabeth.

With every passing moment, I was becoming a horrible monster and I had no idea how I would face myself when finally I would have to tell her the truth.

I had to gather that strength somehow.

Chapter – 7

Never Easy to Face Your Demons

[Summer '07]

(One Week Ago)

What was she; that girl, Viola Harris? What was she to me? She was not a person, not for me at least. She was a soul, a light or perhaps just an utter figment of my imagination. Why did I write for her? My poems or descriptions had always been metaphysical; abstract. She was myfirst muse for writing, who could be seen or touched. She was not the first girl I had felt this way for. But she was the first to drive my mind crazy. I always knew where to stop thinking about something, when to give rest to my sanity. But she compelled me to smile whenever I thought of her; or get restless every time I saw her smile vividly in my mind's eye, over and over and over again. Was she something I was supposed to chase after? Was she someone I was supposed to find my meaning in? Was she the one I was to dedicate my actuality to?

Or maybe, I was just being stagy. It was better for me to stop thinking about her and concentrate on other important things. But, how could I; especially when my mind was all over her voice when she told me where to find her; and her expressions when she was leaving, while secretly wanting me to meet her again.

"Hey Jay, this came for you," Aarav handed me a letter."Some young dude gave it to the security guard of the building and told him it's urgent."

I quickly got off my bed and tore the envelopeopen. I knew who the young boy was and I knew what it could be regarding.

"Whoa man, is everything alright? Why do you seem so freaked out?" Aarav asked me as I read the letter with nervous eyes and shivering hands.

When I finished reading, I gave it to him to read and understand.

Dear Jay,

By the time you read this letter I'd be gone. I am sorry I did not tell you about my illness, but you must understand that I did not want you to worry for me. I lived a happy life and I'm going peacefully. I knew that someday, this moment would arrive for you to come back home one last time. Your parents' funeral was the last day you were here and I know you still have not forgiven me for what I did.But I want you to know, I just wanted you to not face that trauma. No child in the world deserves something as distressing and atrocious as that.

In the end, I just wish… I hope… that someday you do find it in your heart to forgive me because I loved you as much as your parents did. And I just wanted you to be safe.

Come back soon. Your parents' gifts are waiting for you.

Your humble servant,

Shravan

"Who is this man? And what is he talking about exactly?" For an outsider like Aarav, the letter was confusing. But I could feel my heart breaking because of it.

"That man used to work for my parents. He and his family were like family for us as well. After my parents' accident, I came here and left everything for him to take care of. He's gone now and it's time for me to go back home to collect what's mine; the gifts from my parents," I replied as I sat back down on the bed. It was hard for me to continue thinking about him.

"Why was he apologizing?"

I did not want to answer that question but as I saw it, Aarav deserved an answer. Not necessarily the truth, just an answer.

"He was really rude to me when I was a little child. That's what he is apologizing for," I answered.

I could see that Aarav did not believe my explanation, but he let it go because he knew that it was something I did not want to talk about.

"I'll help you pack," he said, the good friend that he was.

I left as soon as I could which I knew was not right. I should've waited and prepared myself for it first. But the more I would've waited, the more I wouldn't have wanted to go back. Hence, I decided to not give myself even the slightest moment to start overthinking and ruin my plans.

I sat in the bus and breathed deeply, occasionally, to keep myself calm. With every passing milestone I was getting more nervous. The distance kept decreasing and the rate of my heartbeat kept increasing.

I got off at the bus stop and there, Shravan's son was waiting for me.

"Hello sir. It's been a lifetime since we saw each other," he greeted me and asked for my bag.

"It's okay." I did not give it to him. "And yes, it's been some 14–15 years. Last time I saw you, I remember you were just three years old."He laughed with me softly. I could see the grief he had regarding his father's death. "I'm sorry to hear about him. Thank you for the letter."

We sat in his car to get to my house. "My father always talked about you. Even though you were just ten when you left, he did not stop remembering you. He told me that you sometimes wrote to him but always urged him not to send a reply. This time, he had to." I knew that he knew what had made me angry with his father and he himself felt apologetic about it. "He gave me your new address and asked me to deliver the letter after his funeral."

"He never wanted me to attend any funeral. It was like his job to keep me away from them." He smiled a little but he understood my point. "Other than my parents, he was the only man I looked up to. And I wish I could've met him one last time."

"I hope you are not angry anymore."

"I was sad; never angry." He stopped the car as soon as I replied.

"We're here," he said softly.

I looked out of my window and there it was; the place of my parents. Your home is supposed to make you feel safe. There should be a kind of warmth and the smell of happiness. Your face should automatically light up when you see it.

I wish I had felt the same way when I got out of the car. I got chills all over my body, in a bad way. I was scared to even look at it. There was no happiness anywhere – just a gloomy obscurity. My hands had started trembling and my heart was pounding. I wanted to turn back and run away.

"I'll give you some time alone. If you need anything, come to my place. You know the way," I heard Shravan's son's voice tell me but I did not even listen to him properly. My mind was fixed on the fact that it was the same place that had made me feel complete once. I recalled how I would come back from playing when I was a little child and would sit with my mother near the gate on the porch, drinking lemonade and watching the sunset. She and I would wait for my father to return from work and I would run and hug him when he came.

Our family was picture perfect. Even as a child, I did not believe in materialistic things. All I cared about was my parents' happiness and their well-being.

My eyes were fixed on the house. It had not changed at all, just a little rusted and pale. The navy blue color of the place had dimmed to grey and the black gates were now red with corrosion.

A blink lasts around 300 to 400 millisccond. That's the mathematical way of saying 'too less.' Every time I blinked, I could see how the house used to be in those 300 to 400 milliseconds. It was indeed too less. No amount of wishing could've changed the reality.

And I had to make my peace with it.

I went inside and switched on the lights. The furniture was covered in white cloth to not let the dust settle. But 14–15 years are a long time,and the dust does find a way to get in through the threads of the cloth.

I looked around the place and tried to keep myself from freaking out. The place reminded me of that awful evening that ruined my reality. I was standing in the same place when my parents had died. I remembered exactly how I was watching Shravan talking to the police officers andthe way he was crying. I did not remember myself crying at that moment. It was all too much for me to take. I remember that I was trying to get my mind off of their deaths but it was hard for me to do that.

After all those years, those memories and feelings were as fresh as they had been.

Two days passed and I finally felt a little better. My definition of 'better' was not happy, but certainly, a little less traumatized. I had to leave the next day so I was preparing myself for it. I always loved sitting on the porch. But this was the first time I was there alone. Regardless of what happened, my home was dear to me. I was feeling as sad as I always felt every time I had to leave for school; annoyingly frustrated. But perhaps it was for the better. I needed to run away from my reminiscences of the past and try to be a happy person.

"Hi!" I heard a voice greeting me. I was stunned when I saw its source.

"Viola!" She was really there.

"What are you doing here, Jay Malhotra?" She walked close to me and again I could feel myself going insane for her. I wanted to reply, but again, words had forgotten how to get out.

"This is my parents' place. I just came to visit. But, what are you doing here?" I asked her.

"My cousin had a baby. I'm here to meet her. I did not know that you lived here." She sat beside me on the porch. Her smile reminded me of my mother's.

"I'm here after fifteen years," I replied. Her gasp told me that she was surprised.

"How can anyone not miss their home? And you stayed away for fifteen years? That is too much." I looked at her had started to get teary. She understood that there was something that had forced me to stay away from this place. "Hey. What happened?"

I broke down as soon as she asked me that question. I started to cry as if I were a little child.

"I'm sorry, I didn't mean to," I said wiping my tears.She wrapped her hands around me. Instead of controlling my tears, I cried even more.

"Whatever it was, it's over now," she whispered in my ear, "Nobody is there to hurt you anymore, only your sadness is. Let go of it and I promise – everything will be perfect."

She made me feel safe. She did not know what it was that I was crying about and she did not care either. She cared about me. It is easy to ask what the problem is and try to find a solution of it. But it's harder to just hold someone when they're broken, till they feel better.

And finally, after a couple of minutes long of sobbing, I was feeling less broken.

"Thank you." I did not know how else to show my gratitude to her.

"Jay."

"Yes?"

"Show me what hurt you."

I paused to take a deep breath. "Okay," I replied.

I took her inside the house. She held my hand firmly as soon as we stepped in. "Can you please switch on the lights?" she requested, and I did.

"This whole place, everything that you're seeing is a part of that agony that I've been through." She did not understand what I was trying to tell her. "My family was happy and I never asked for anything other than their happiness. My mother was a piano player in her youth. She had won countless competitions. My father was the owner of a cloth mill and he met my mother in one of her competitions. He used to say that it was love at first sight. My parents were happy. They never fought, never argued and never hurt each other. They had that unspoken connection which is rare in this world. But there was something they hid from me because I was a child. Sometimes I heard my mother cry and my father comforting her. I would sneak up to them but he would kiss my head and request me to go back to sleep. One evening, I heard him talking to a psychiatrist. My mother was mentally ill. I don't remember what was wrong with her but she would only stay okay when she was on her medication. They loved me very much; enough not to stress me with her problem. So nobody ever told me what was happening."

Viola held my hand even firmly. I could feel her fear. She looked deeply into my eyes which revealed my truth. "What happened then?"

I looked back at her and somehow, she gave me the courage to complete the story. "One night, I was woken upby the sound of my parents yelling and found mymother looking bewildered. My father was trying his best to assure her that everything would be okay, but this time she was not ready to listen to him."

It was getting hard for me to speak. "She-she had a knife, in her hand. And…and she came close to me to kiss my head. But my father stopped her and-and told her to stay away from me. I was just a child; I did not know what was happening. I got really scared. My mother tried to free herself from my father's hold but he did not let go. He should've let her go. She was my mother. She wouldn't have hurt me."

"Jay what happened?" Viola asked me again, trying her best to keep me strong.

"My mother stabbed my father in the stomach. She stabbed him. And…and he-he died. He died right there." I pointed near the couch. "My mother knew what she had done. She started crying at her mistake, apologizing to the lifeless body of my father. I was too afraid. I tried to talk to her but she thought I was judging her. I just asked her what she had done. But she got really scared as well. She came close to me and hugged me tightly; telling me how sorry she was that she couldn't be a good mother to me. And before I could say anything, she stabbed herself too."

All my energy drained. It's said that relating something that has happened, out loud, makes it even more real. That same thing happened with me. I fell on the floor, finally facing reality. Viola sat down with me there and started to stroke my hair. "My parent's servant, he died a few days ago. He was like family to us. He and his wife had taken care of my mother whenever my father was not there. He spread the word that they had died in a car accident so that no one would know about my mother's condition. He died thinking I was angry with him because he did not let me be there at my parents' funeral. He thought that I might not be okay if I had stayed; I was already too overwhelmed with emotions. So he sent me to the city where I stayed with his brother's family for some time. I never returned because I was scared to even think about that night, let alone be in the same room again. And to answer your question, that's what happened." For the first time I had shared my story with someone.

I was waiting for her to say something. But she quietly kept looking down. Then she turned to me and smiled. "Tell me where your mother's piano is." I was surprised that she wanted to know that but I took her to the study, where the piano was.

She took the cloth off of it and sat down on the bench. "It's been a while." She looked at the notes that were there and inadvertently chose the song that was my mother's favorite.

Your eyes speak to mine; saying what you didn't say, let them talk,

Your lips take me on a journey; beyond all the heavens, let me walk;

Your touch sparks my veins; through my heart, which was almost a rock,

You can have my life; can even have my soul, no breaking any locks.

So stay here with me; stay as beautiful as you are; because I'm going crazy,

Let me lie in your lap; let me feel your warmth, because I'm sleeping like a baby;

Life is driving me insane; this world is trying to kill me; please don't ever leave me,

I've been walking alone till now; with chains in my feet, now I've found the key.

I don't know if you love me; need me, or if all this for you is fake,

I don't know if I'm really the one; made for you, or it's just my faith;

But you should know; and keep in your mind, that you truly are my soul mate,

My heart has chosen your arms; to die in, and to be with you till my last date.

So I'm praying; for this moment to stop, so I could be with you all eternity,

I'm broken; touch me with your lips, because only you know the real me;

Let's forget the people; let's forget their rules, let's make a life with love and no cease,

Because you, and my love only you, can bring my heart, soul and life some peace.

I sat beside her on the bench with my heart pouring out of my chest and she looked at me with a smile.

"You didn't have to tell me everything. I know it was hard," she said.

"I know I didn't have to. But I wanted to," I whispered. I wanted to say so much to her but I did not know how to begin. I was constantly begging time to stop so that she could stay this way forever in front of me. I leaned in close to her and so did she. And then there was a moment when the sparks started to fly, as our lips touched. She had stopped playing and had held me instead, tightly in her arms and I held her tightly as well. It was quite apparent that I was falling for her, but her touch had made me realize she was falling for me too.

She requested me to take the piano, my mother's gift to me and my father's Chevrolet Camaro back with me and I agreed. For the first time in fifteen years I looked at my house with a smile on my face. That placewould always have the memories of the demise of my parents; but also of how Viola, found the real Jay.

Chapter – 8

His Turn to Fall off that Cliff

[Summer '07]

(Three Hours Ago)

"Could you help me with something Jay?" Viola asked me as she and I washed the car that once belonged to my father, but was now mine.

I just nodded my head; my mind was too busy thinking about my father.

"My mother is coming to the city around the start of next month and I want you to meet her." I heard her and my whole body started shivering.

"What? Why?" I asked her. I was not even sure what she and I were. I didn't know if we were in love or she just liked me. It was too soon to meet her mother.

She came close to me and held my hand. "Jay, my mother is the most important person in my life. I have never had friends or close relatives. It has been just us against the world. Ever since my father left her, she's been really cranky. It's been ten years since that event but she remembers it like yesterday. She even cries sometimes when she thinks I am asleep."

"But Viola, how am I supposed to help her in any way?" I did not understand what she wanted from me.

"You don't understand anything my boy," Aarav said from behind. "She's setting you up with her mother. She wants you to be her stepdad." He said as he took a bite of the carrot in his hand.

"Okay first of all, I told you Jay it was the worst idea to invite this weird guy to wash the car with us. He has been no help at all. And secondly, no I do not want him to be my stepdad you dumb head," Viola replied. "I just want her to meet you once. So that she knows that not everyone is bad. There are still some good guys left in the world." She looked into my eyes as she always did and I understood her feelings.

"Okay Viola. I'd love to meet her." I kissed her cheek softly. She was really happy with my reply, so happy that she hugged me tightly.

"I've to go now." She was still really happy. "Thank you so much for doing this. And you dumb head, bye." She bid farewell and left for her place.

Telling Viola about what happened with my parents had been the right thing to do. She showed me how I could be happy even after every bit of hurt that I had been through. She made me tell Aarav the truth too. And he was as supportive as she was. They both had that love/hate relationship. They made fun of each other, but both of them were thankful to each other for being in my life.

"She's amazing Jay." Aarav approached me when Viola left. "But so is someone else." He was referring to Amelia. "It'll be too late if you let things continue this way."

He was right again. It was time to finish things with her. "You're right Aarav. It's time to end my relationship with

Amelia. And you know what, I'll go right now." Viola had given me the courage to do the right thing as soon as possible. And the present is always the right time.

I called her to ask if I could see her and she agreed. I could hear the love she had for me in her voice. I did not stop being in contact with her. I constantly asked her how she was feeling and if she had been taking her medications properly or not. She would always want to hear me say that I loved her, but I knew I had my limits too.

On my way to the hospital, I hadproblem breathing. I was going to do something really horrible and there was no way to avoid it. To be exact, I had already done something horrible. I was just going to apologize for my doing it.

As soon as I saw her I realized how atrocious I had been with someone as pure as her. I did not look at her even once while telling her the truth. She kept showing me how alright she was with everything I was telling her, but I knew the truth. She wasdying from inside. I wanted to get on my knees and beg her to forgive me; that would've been the appropriate way to apologize. But I was so shameless that I did not do that. I just plainly told her that I did not love her, that I had someone else in my life and that I was sorry. I was the world's worst person at that moment. She did say it was okay. She did smile. But I understood the truth. I just had no way of letting her know how apologetic I was.

I realized that I was like my mother in her last moments. I had stabbed someone in the heart and was apologizing for it. There was no forgiveness for me. No matter what I had told her.

People would've called me immature for doing something like this. They would've told me that I should've just comforted her as a friend would. But they did not care as I did. They did not want her to get better as I did. They did not think of her happiness as I did. I knew since the beginning that I shouldn't have played with her feelings the way I had. But my intentions had never been wrong. I just wanted her to be happy.

Not that it mattered anyway.

***

It wasn't like he and I were in a relationship, or that we chose to be exclusive. But then why was I so bothered that he was in a relationship with someone else? I was debating whether I should call him or not when I finally decided that it was better to talk to him about it.

"Meet me near the cattle ranch," I told him as soon as he picked up my call.

"Is it something urgent? It's raining" he said me; trying to make up an excuse to not meet me. I should've known him for what he really was.

I controlled my rage as much as I could. "I won't repeat myself. Come there as soon as possible," I said and I hung up.

I had to hurt him. I had to humiliate him. I was giving him all my feelings and he had turned out to be a double dater. He was cheating on that sick girl with me; or maybe it was the other way around. All I knew was that I needed him to tell me the truth so that I could tell him how pathetic a human being he was.

My mind was on the verge of bursting when I saw him come. I had different scenarios planned in my mind on how to play the situation and the best one was that I would show myself to be calm and allow him to humiliate himself.

"Is everything okay, Viola?" he asked to me.

I wanted to keep my anger to myself but I couldn't control it. I slapped him hard across his face.

"You're a liar and a cheat, Jay Malhotra. I should've known that you were no different from all those bastards who play with the feelings of everyone they know. I heard everything that you and Aarav were talking about when you thought I had left. But fortunately, I had forgotten my keys near the car. I heard you say that you were going to break up with Amelia. And I know who she is. She's that poor girl who is sick and is in hospital. I feel worse for her than I feel for myself."

I did not realize when the tears had begun to fall. I thought that being in the rain would not reveal that I was crying, but I could see on his face that he knew that I was. "Now, I'm sure everything that you told me was just a lie. I'm sure you lied about your parents too; because that's what you are, a liar."

I wanted to leave; I was done saying everything that I had to. But I wanted to hear him say something for himself.

"You're right Viola. I really am just a liar. I lied to you, I lied to Amelia and I lied to myself when I thought my actions would not have consequences. But you know what? I do want to clarify something to you. The only reason I told Amy that I had 'strong feelings' for her was because she is sick and is deeply in love with me. I did not want to break her heart and in my stupidity, I let her believe I was her boyfriend. She's nothing less than an angel and I'll never forgive myself for doing that to her. As far as you are concerned, well I'm sure you will not believe anything that I say, but I still want you to listen to me."

My heart rate had started to rise and I was panting.

He continued, "Since I saw you in that subway I've been questioning myself as to whom you actually are. I could not come to a conclusion. Sometimes I would say you're just a girl I like very much and at other times, I would be in awe of the way my soul wants to belong to you. My words may seem untrue to you. You may think that I'm lying to get you to be with me again. It's okay; don't be with me; because I want you to be happy. You might think that I don't deserve another chance from you. Maybe I don't. But Viola, you are not just another girl to me. You're my savior. I feel you don't exist in real life, you're just a part of the dream that I'm seeing because that's how my life feels after meeting you; surreal. Everywhere I go, I hear you say my name. No matter where I look, I see you smiling at me. I have literally filled an entire notebook just with my thoughts about you. But you know what, screw everything I just said. Just listen to what I'm going to say now. Love is not just about togetherness and making each other happy. It's also about knowing. And Viola Harris, you know the real Jay Malhotra. I can go on pretending in front of the whole world – but make me strip off my skin and show you my soul. Just believe me when I say you're the only person in the whole world that I've ever been in love with. And you're the only one who knows the real me."

I had started to tremble when he said the first words. But I suddenly felt warmth in my heart. I didn't know how, but I could see that he was telling the truth. I saw veracity in his eyes and it was that he was truly in love with me.

"I'm sorry for everything. Bye." He turned around to leave. But I did not want him to. I was not so cruel. I held his hand and stopped him from leaving. He turned around and I saw that he was teary-eyed again.

And suddenly, I melted.

I couldn't take it anymore. I was with him in his struggle. I was there even if I did not want to. I pulled him close to me and pressed my lips against his with all the love I had in my soul. He just made the moment perfect when he held me tightly against his body. Neither of us cared that we were getting wet or that we both had tears in our eyes. I could taste his tears on his lips and I knew he could taste mine as well. It just added to the magnificence of that moment.

The sound of the rain was like applause for our souls that were together in love. It was the first time that I did not hate the rain. Nor did I hate him anymore. An hour ago I wanted to destroy his being. But now, in each other's arms, we knew we belonged there.

A month passed in a snap. I had never felt so speechless before in my life. His every word, every smile, every kiss and every touch made me feel wordless. I did not understand how it could be so easy for him to be so perfect; and like the excellence he typified, he never accepted that fact. He always said that I changed his life, but I was not sure of that. I think, in the process of being changed by me, he modified me. And I knew, that, was the magic of love.

Since my father had left my mother, she had stopped trusting any male figure. He had broken her completely. It was a miracle that she did not turn suicidal. She had just me and I had just her. I think in some way, she made me believe in her thinking too. That was why I was always reluctant to be with any guy. But this person completely eliminated any kind of fear that I had regarding love or relationships.

I had been preparing Jay to meet my mother. He was really nervous but I believed in him. I was sure he would change my mother's thinking as well.

"I still don't think it's such a good idea Viola," he said as I dressed him up according to me. He looked as charming as anyone can be.

"And I still think she's setting you up with her mother," Aarav said. He had been helping me sort through Jay's macabre wardrobe to find something decent. "Look at the signs; she wants you to meet her because apparently 'you are a nice guy'. She has been constantly telling you what her mother likes and what she doesn't so you could make a great first impression. And she wants you to look perfect for the, as you might have guessed, first date with her."

Jay looked at me with wide open eyes. "Fine, I agree it does look like that's what I'm trying to do but you, boy…" I squeezed Jay's shoulder, "Don't you believe anything this idiot has to say."

Jay just smiled at my words with Aarav. He loved it that his best friend and his girlfriend did not hate each other.

"Dude, why are you even doing this if you don't think it's a good idea?" Aarav asked Jay.

I looked him for a reply. He turned around and smiled at me. "She thinks it's a good idea. I trust her decisions." He kissed me on my cheek.

I smiled back at him. Every second that I spent with him made my belief stronger – that he was, in every way, the one for me.

"Oh the sappy, romantic crap again! Ugh Jay. I mean seriously, ugh. Just listen to me, ugh. I'll repeat myself, ugh.

Ugh. Just, ugh." Aarav's words did not bother either of us. "I think I'm going to vomit my intestines out. And again…" Jay cut him in between.

"I got it Aarav, ugh." Jay's words made Aarav grin.

"Non importé," Aarav approached us. "I know she will love Jay. And I'm sure she'll love her very much, until she dies. And even beyond that, till the end of time." He grinned again.

"For a second, I actually believed he got better but of course, that is not possible," I said to Jay and they both hugged. Jay and I, we both knew that in his weird way, he was wishing us the best of luck and it made us really happy.

We sat in Jay's car and I could sense his nervousness. He kept making faces but did not want me to see him doing that. "Jay, what's wrong?"

He looked at me and smiled. "You look really lovely." So simple, yet every inch of my body quivered in happiness.

I wanted to tell him that I was falling for him; I wanted to say it out loud. But I wanted the occasion to be perfect. I couldn't just say it out of the blue.

"There, right at the corner. She told me she'd be inside," I told Jay and he stopped the car. I looked into his eyes and smiled. "Go melt her heart. Trust me, you can."

If only he knew how amazing he looked. It was not something he needed to be nervous about. We got out and I held his arm. "Let's do this." He smiled at me and I smiled back. Finally, he was confident enough and that spark in his eyes gave me the confidence too.

We got inside the restaurant and my mother was sitting there, drinking herbal tea. "Hi, mom," I greeted her from the door. She looked at me and gave that proud smile she always did. But then, I did not know why, her smile started to fade.

I hugged her tightly. “I missed you so much my baby,” she said to me.

“Oh mom me too,” I kissed her cheek. Then I remembered. “Oh I’m so sorry. Mom this is Jay,who I was talking about.” He shook my mother’s hand awkwardly and I realized she was not smiling for real. It was phony.

We sat down and talked for a little while. Jay was trying his best not to seem nervous but he still was. I held his hand from under the table and felt him becoming calm.

“My mother’s an architect,” I told Jay. “She is one of the best across the country.” Jay was not the only one on test. I did not show it to him, but I was too. I had to show how good my mother was.

“Stop it, Viola. I have always told you not to praise me in front of people. It makes me seem arrogant and proud.” My mother said to me and I laughed. Jay realized that my mother was being rude.

“I’m sure whatever Viola is saying about you is completely true ma’am,” Jay said to her with his signature innocent smile.

But my mother had different plans. She entirely ignored what he said and stared at him. “What are you pursuing in SAU Jay? I mean, other than my daughter.” She laughed.

“Mom,” I looked at her, trying to hint to her not to do that.

“That’s okay Viola,” Jay laughed uneasily. “I’m a student of MA in English ma’am.”

“Alright, and what are your plans after this?”

"I think I'm going to go for a PhD and then I'd like to teach."

"Teaching?" my mother repeated. "Do you think it'll be enough to support a family?" she asked him.

"Mom stop, you are embarrassing me," I whispered it to her.

"It's okay, Viola. Ma'am I think…" Before Jay could say anything she spoke.

"Tell me about your parents Jay. Viola told me that they died. You know the town you live in; it's the same place where my niece's husband lived all his life. And his parents told me there had been a murder of a man in the neighborhood. A woman had killed her husband and then killed herself. What was their last name, I don't remember?"

"Mom, what is wrong with you? Stop it now. I'm so sorry Jay." I held his hand tightly.

"It's okay Viola," he whispered.

My mother got off her chair and everyone around us looked at her. "Listen to me you son of a psycho. Just because you can write silly, pathetic poems for my daughter and lure her in your cheap style does not mean you can take her for granted. I have seen people like you. One of them ruined my life and I would never let you ruin my daughter's."

Jay looked down and did not say anything. I knew he could've but he chose not to just because she was my mother. He let her insult him and he suffered through it.

"Mother!" I yelled. "I came here to show you how marvelous this person has made my life but you don't care about it for even a second. Not everyone has luck like you.

You had a pitiable life – that does not mean I will as well." I was standing too. "Be happy he kept quiet for my sake; because even if he had said something I wouldn't have stopped him." I held Jay's hand and left the place.

Jay still did not say anything during the ride home. I kept cursing my mother and apologizing to him but he was completely silent. I did not know my mother knew about his parents' truth or that she had researched about him. She must have called my cousin and asked if her in-laws knew anything about him. But regardless of what she said, I was the one who was at fault. I had been forcing him to meet her thinking he would be able to clear my mother's clouded judgment. He did what he could. I wished I had done something more.

We stopped at my apartment. "Goodnight,"he said without looking at me.

"Jay," I wanted to say so much but did not know where to start. Then my feelings for him hit me suddenly. "Take me dancing," I said to him.

"I'm not in the mood Viola, I'm sorry," he said.

I went close to him and kissed his cheek. "I really want to dance with you," I whispered and he reluctantly agreed.

We turned around and he stopped at a club. But that was not the place I wanted us to go. "I'll give you the directions, you just drive" I said to him with a chuckle.

After a while he understood where I was taking him.He did not need me to tell him anymore. We reached the gates of Reindeer Gardens and got out of the car. I held his hand and led him to the place where we had met for the first time, near the lake, beside the cherry blossom tree. The night sky made the scene even more placid. It was like the whole world wanted to swing with us right there, right then.

I played a recording of me playing piano that he had on his phone and took off my shoes. He loved the way I played and always gave an intentional smile during my sessions.

"May I have the honor of dancing with you sir?" I bowed in front of him. My sundress had already started dancing. And for the first time since meeting my mom, he smiled.

He put his hand in mine and we swayed softly together. Neither of us knew how to dance. But at that point only we mattered. He kept my left hand near his heart and pulled me close by my waist. I looked into his eyes which sparkled brightly. He was smiling like nothing had happened.

"I wrote something for you," he said, making me excited.

She asks me, "What am I to you?" with a smile,

I asked "Do you so want to know?" as she's a child.

She looks at me with eagerness in her Godly eyes,

I tell her, "Oh baby, this one look as a yes will suffice."

Like what air is to a man drowning under water,

And how important is her mother to a daughter;

What the sun is to a man freezing in terrible cold,

And a bite of the sweetest candy for a three year old.

How a man cannot live without his beating heart,

The same way, I don't want us to ever be apart;

How the stars cannot be seen in the sky in the day,

You're as important as night, that's what I want to say.

You are the reason I exist, you really are my 'everything';

Just your thoughts are so mesmerizing and heart melting.

I can go on and on about what you are to me, my soul,

But the last two words said everything already as a whole.

"I love you so much Viola." I fell for him all over again as soon as he said those words. I wanted to say the same but I did not have the strength to do that yet. I just put my head on his chest as we kept swaying softly under the falling petals, with love in our hearts and contentment in our minds. He was everything I ever wanted or needed. And that smile of mine was a validation of that fact as I brushed my face on his chest to wipe the little tear I had in my eyes and held him tightly. He kissed my head and said, "I'm always here. I promise." And I was complete.

Chapter – 9

The Insincere Promise

[The Present]

Jay stood there silently, watching the little kids throw rocks into the lake, trying to bounce theirs. Beside the lake was the bench he had sat on when he had seen Viola for the first time. "So much has changed since then,"he thought to himself. He had changed, she changed and the way he lived had changed. He did not pay attention to the fact that he desperately missed those days, but he knew that he did. He missed the person he used to be. He missed his happiness, his personality, his authenticity that he had once had, and of course, he missed the love he in his heart.

"Good evening professor," one of his new students greeted him.

Jay looked at him and tried to remember his name. "Good evening. Saransh Shah, aren't you?" he asked him.

"I honestly did not expect you to remember my name, sir."Saransh was handsome. Jay had never found a man beautiful. Everyone looked the same to him. But he understood this difference when he saw every girl who passed by, looking at Saransh and smiling. Perhaps it was his amazing jawline or maybe his blue eyes. His spotless face and muscular body added allure to his overall charm. Unlike Jay who seemed weak, tired and depressed.

"I'm good with names. How may I help you Mr. Shah?" Jay never really liked meeting his students out of the university. It already felt weird for him to pretend to be someone else while teaching. Meeting them outside was too uncomfortable.

"Oh, nothing professor; I just saw you here so I thought I'd meet you. Beautiful weather, isn't it?" Saransh wanted to talk to Jay, but his professor was just not interested.

"It is. But, I know you want something. Tell me, what is it?" Jay cut to the chase. It was always difficult for Jay's students to hide things from him. And Saransh was not the first who came to him with some problem and tried to beat about the bush.

He felt a little embarrassed with Jay's sudden question. "To be honest professor, I don't exactly need something. I just have a question," Saransh replied awkwardly.

"Go on."

"Professor, how do I fix someone who is completely broken and does not want to get fixed?" he asked.

His question made Jay's body go weak. Suddenly, he could see himself dancing with Viola near the lake,to the sound of her playing the piano. He knew he was imagining it, but this was enough to mentally scar him all over again.

"Is everything alright, sir? You look like you've seen a ghost." Saransh asked as he saw Jay turn pale. He did not know that Jay had almost really seen a ghost.

"I need to go. I had forgotten something," Jay said to him and turned to leave.

"But professor, how does someone fix those broken beyond repair?" Saransh really wanted to know the answer.

"You can't," Jay replied without looking at his student, and left. Saransh was a little irritated but this was not the first time that Jay had acted weird. No matter how hard Jay tried to be someone else in the classroom while teaching, he was not perfect at it. Something or the other always hinted that he was acting.

No one knew the reason.

Sometimes your heart cries,

When the pain is on the rise;

You try to keep a straight look,

And hide the pages of your book;

Comprising the story of your woe,

But still deep down you so know;

No sum of words will ever suffice,

How sometimes your heart cries.

Sometimes my heart cries,

Suddenly all of my joy dies;

My soul gets scared so much,

Feels like my body was touched;

By the ghost of agony and distress,

I lust for depression, my mistress;

There is loneliness behind my smile

Because sometimes my heart cries

[Summer '08]

A year changes so much. It does not seem so sometimes, but if you start noticing the minute details, you start realizing the changes. I tried my best to make it up to Amelia. I took care of her in every way possible. After a while she started to seem to get better physically. And she got back to the way she had been with me. The only difference was my interactions with her had changed her in an unseen way. It was not something everyone could see, but I had started to get an idea about what it was. She nursed disappointment in her heart regarding me. No amount of apology or making up could have changed what I did to her and as anordinary human being, I had stopped trying.

"Congratulations on those great marks," I said to her when I visited her place.

"You call those marks great? If that is great then yours are out of this world. You got the best marks in the entire history of the university. I should be the one congratulating you," she praised me.

I never knew how to accept compliments gracefully. I always got really shy and awkward,and responded with a big smile on my face. "I try." That's all I could reply.

She smiled with me, "So, how does it feel to leave for Oxford?" She was more excited about it than me. But I kept it low just because I did not want to jinx it.

"I'm having mixed feelings about it all, honestly." I did not want to describe everything.

"Oh you're here. Viola is waiting for you outside. And this is for you," Aarav entered the room with a bowl of soup.

"I have to go now Amelia," I hugged her. I knew what she was going to say. "Yes, I promise I'll be in touch and I'll meet you as soon as I'll get back." She laughed. I could see she had a tear in her eye but before I could say anything, she wiped it off. "And…" I had to add something. "I'm really sorry for whatever happened."

"It's okay Jay. It always is." She held my hand. "All the best Jay Malhotra, I hope you have an amazing life there. Slay all your colleagues," she said with a smile and I left.

***

"Did you tell him about that evening?" I asked Amelia as soon as Jay left. She had her head down and did not say anything. She was crying and I could see her tears falling on the bed.

(A year ago)

I was on my way to check up on Amelia as Jay had asked me to. My mind was busy hoping that she would be okay. The things Jay had told me about her were too nice.And being told by the person you're deeply in love with that theywere only pretending to be with you, paralyzes your senses. Your soul then is barely alive, just enough to feel every kind of pain it can experience.

When I got close to Amelia's room, the chaos there scared me. Doctors and nurses were rushing inside the room. My heart started pounding when I saw them taking her to the ICU on a stretcher.

"Excuse me, please, ma'am. Tell me what happened to her?" I begged a nurse.

"Do not worry sir, she will be okay but only if you let us do our work," she replied and rushed inside the ICU.

I had been calling Jay constantly but his phone was switched off and the voicemail was full. I was really furious with him but my first priority was to make sure that Amy was okay.

After a long wait for about an hour, I finally got a chance to see her. "Hey Amy, this is Aarav." I entered her room.

"Aarav, yes, hello; it's nice to finally meet you properly." Her smile was peaceful, but she looked very pale.

We talked for an hour and I did not feel anything but happiness. "I'm sorry I can't reach Jay at the moment. I've been trying but his phone is off," I told her and he held my arm.

"Please don't tell him," she requested me.

"After what he did to you, he deserves to know."

"You don't understand. It'll kill him with guilt to know what happened after he left. He's not a bad person. He just made a mistake. He told me the truth as soon as possible because he cared for me. If it had beensomeone else, someone terrible and someone who takes people for granted, they would've kept me in the dark. It's a miracle I'm still alive, but I would've died then."

It was fascinating that she still judged Jay to be good person. She was right. If he were someone treacherous he would've kept her in the dark and would've made fake promises. Those people deserved guilt, Jay didn't.

"He said he is going to propose to Viola soon, to ask her to marry him." That's all she could say. She had kept a straight face in front of Jay but as soon as he was gone she broke down.

"Come on Amy, cheer up." I put an arm around her and rubbed her shoulder. "You need to stay strong. Besides, Elizabeth might come up. You wouldn't want revealwhat happened to your'Seigneur', would you?" And she smiled.

***

It was our one year anniversary. I stepped outside Amelia's apartment and my Viola was waiting for me there in all her grandeur. Her eyes had a kind of seduction in them that always made my mind go crazy. I went up to her and she kissed me on the cheek as I held her in my arms.

"Happy anniversary my love!" she whispered in my ear and held me tightly. She and I have been the happiest a couple can be.

We both smiled and I kissed her nose. "Let's go."

She loved long drives. So I gave in to her wish. I took the longest route possible home and she made sure to let me know how much she enjoyed it. The car's stereo was playing all her favorite songs and she moved to the music all the way.

We reached my apartment and the surprise began. She had already asked me to not do anything lavish and that just a homemade dinner would be okay. And I did exactly as she had requested, just in a different way.

I took her up to the roof where it all was. There was a picnic cloth for us to sit on with white wine and salad on one side. To keep the wine chilled, I had frozen grapes in an icebox. Above us were dimly lit bulbs of different colors to give us the feeling of rainbows. I was a little nervous about everything but seeing her reaction made me feel all good about my setting.

"My good lord, oh baby this is all so perfect!" she said with her hands on her cheeks. When I did not reply, she turned around.

"I have a fantasy, of a perfect day;
Looking into each other's eyes as we lay
Under the golden sky and the setting sun;
In front of the ocean, the water seeming like rum.

I request my mind, to think of something flawless;
But sadly it's gazing at you and made me speechless.
Now that I think of it, it's your entire mistake,
Being perfect for you is like a piece of cake.

You fill my heart with love and romance,
And I hope God gives me a chance
To create a new beautiful word for you,
To describe the whole of you

Because no language yet could do that,
And no other human being ever can;
I know my feelings will create something as pure,
After all there's a part of you inside of my core.

You said, "I love you" and my heart suddenly
Skipped several beats and it felt heavenly;
We leaned in and your lips touched mine,
The ocean stopped moving, so did the time.
That feeling can't be brought into words,

But if that moment was the end of the world

I wouldn't have cared for any other thing,

As I have had my share of the eternal heavenly bliss.

I wish I could tell you how much I love you,

I wish I knew how much I want to be with you;

But even infinity seems insignificant and eternity too,

Just want our love to make us the perfect two.

I pray to God to make this fantasy come alive,

As you baby, are the one and only love of my life;

You have no idea what your significance is for me,

You really are the one for someone and that somebody's me."

I had accomplished my mission. She was figuratively swaying in the air with happiness. She jumped into my arms and I swung her around while she kissed me with all her love.

We talked, laughed, kissed, made fun of and threw food at each other. It was all too ordinary. Nothing was over the top or too extravagant, yet it was more beautiful than being in a swank hotel for a candle light dinner.

She lied on my back looking at the sky as I drank my wine and stroked her hair. "Jay?" she spoke as I put a berry in her mouth.

"Yes my love?"

"I love you so much."

It took me a minute to believe that she had finally said those words. It was her first time. I just smiled and looked at her with love. "You took your time to tell me that," I said to her and she smiled shyly while biting on the berry.

"I wanted to say it since the day we met at Reindeer Gardens, but I was waiting for a special day. And trust me when I tell you, nothing can be more special than this moment. Us, our love, stars, beauty, serenity…I don't want anything else; ever."

If I could, I would marry her right then. She completed me, she made me feel home. She was not just the girl I loved; she was the one I lived for. She was the one I continued to exist for and I wanted her to be the person I would remain alive for.

She got up and held my hands. "I love you. I love you more than I understood that I couldlove. I don't want to love anything or anyone other than you and I never will. You're at an entirely different level in my heart and I just love you even more because it's the best thing I have ever done or I ever can." She started to sob. "Don't forget me when you go there please. And don't you ever presume I won't be thinking of you here because I promise, I will be, all the time. Don't let anyone influence you for anything. I know how nice you are. Don't let anyone take you for granted. And, please, keep being in love with me." She had tears in her eyes.

And so did I

"Viola Harris, I love you. I don't know what else to say because you make me completely speechless."

"Jay Malhotra, you don't need to say anything else. Those words say everything that your heart wants you to." She kissed me as passionately as possible. Her man was leaving and neither of us was happy about it.

I woke up in my room with Viola lying in my arms. I looked around and found a notebook that she had given me.

We must have gotten drunk and scribbled all over it because I found twenty pages with 'Jay *heart* Viola' scrawled all over. I got up and looked at her. She did not know how godly she looked when asleep. I did not want to leave her. If I could have, I would have stayed with her for all eternity.

I got off the bed and realized that it was almost time for my flight. I was about to wake Aarav up, but he was already ready to drop me at the airport, with a smile.

On our way, he gave me a long speech, telling me what to eat and what not to, how to live and whom to talk to; but my mind was fixed on my Viola. My heart was playing symphonies of love and I wanted to go right back to her.

"Alright, off you go now," Aarav said to me, trying not to cry. Without saying a word I hugged him tightly. "Hey now, don't make me cry Shriyut," he teased.

"You're my only family Aarav. I can never thank you enough. I have always wanted to say this to my father, but I lost him. So I say this to you; I promise I will make you proud. When I return, you will have a huge smile on your face with pride. You will always be my best friend Aarav. Just miss me when I'm gone," I said and he just nodded with eyes filled with tears,a smile on his face.

It was the beginning of another part of my life and the end of the one I was living. If only my parents were there to see me. Everything I was doing, it was all for them and to honor their memories. Everything good that had happened to me was their blessing; everything bad was their way of teaching me.

My excitement was of the little child in me and I loved it.

Chapter – 10

When I'll be Dead, my Love

[The Present]

Jay reached his apartment from the university and found Estella waiting outside. It had been a week since he had seen her,after the last time they had met in his classroom. He knew he had been messing a lot with her and he did want to make up to her.

"Ms. Hudson. I didn't expect you here," he said to her.

"I have a story, for the play," she replied coldly.

"Congratulations! What is it about?"

She stared at him, trying to get an answer. "Dilemma."

Jay did not understand what she meant but he trusted her instincts. "Alright then, would you like to go upstairs? We will talk about it."

Estella did not seem interested in his proposal. "It's okay. I'll see you at university some time; we will talk about it then. I've to go now. Goodnight, sir."

Jay had seen herthe night before again, as it was a Thursday – at around midnight,holding a rose. This time she had not covered herself up. She openly showed her face and even looked up at Jay's balcony, where he had been standing with a glass of bourbon in his hand. She felt violated by his intrusion in her life. There was a reason she did not want people to know about this. Laurel and Kathryn knewand it was more than enough.

"Estella," Jay called out and she stopped. "We're going to Opera's tomorrow night. It'll be a good change of scene."

Estella did not want to go. But the problem was, he had not asked her, he just told her to be ready. Before she could say anything, Jay spoke again.

"I'll pick you up at 9." He again, did not 'ask'. Estella was wondering at the arrogance in him. But then she remembered Viola and had a change of heart.

"Sure," she replied and continued on her path.

(Two Months Ago)

"What exactly has happened to you Essie? We are your friends! For God's sake just stop shutting us out!" Laurel shouted as she and Kathryn barged into my apartment.

I did not even look at them; my eyes were set on the bird outside the window. "Have you ever wondered how many people you have seen for the last time?" I asked them.

"What the hell! Why are you so morbid suddenly?" Kathryn was freaking out. "Look Essie, I know you have suffered an incredibly shattering loss. And so does Laurel. But we care about you too much. We cannot let you stay this way," she squatted near my legs.

I needed time to grieve, and they should've understood. But they were forcing me to get normal too soon. It had been just days after Agastya's passing. I couldn't have just moved on so easily. "I just need to be alone," I told them straight.

I expected Laurel to be understanding; she was always the mature one among us. But she was angry with me. "This isn't right Essie. You know what, do what you want. I won't say anything anymore.

"Can't you just let me be on my own for some time Laurel? Why on earth is it so necessary for me to get better so easily? Do you even understand what has happened? He was proposing to me. Agastya wanted to marry me. He wanted to spend the rest of his days with me. And just before he could ask me to marry him, he…" I had started to choke. My voice was cracking and my eyes had tears. "I'm urging to the both of you. Please, please let me take my time. I don't have anything left other than his memories."

Kathryn got up. "I can't imagine how it feels to lose the one you love Essie. It's impossible to even think of a life without Laurel in it…oh God." She stopped.

"What? Laurel? What do you mean?" I asked her.

Both of them kept looking at each other. I saw happiness mixed with sadness in their eyes. "Uh well, Laurel and-and I, we are engaged."

My eyes opened as wide as possible. My best friends were in love with each other and not just that, they were engaged to each other. "What the…" Laurel cut me in between.

"I know what you're thinking. I know all your questions Essie. But give us a chance to explain."

"Please do that, yes," I was stunned.

"To be honest, it sort of just happened. We did not plan to be lesbians I promise you and we did not want to hide anything from you either. It's just our timing wasn't right," she said and Kathryn held her hand.

I had always been okay with homosexuality but my best friends closing up to each other seemed like a joke to me; a bit creepy joke.

"Remember my birthday? You and Agastya hit off so Laurel and I were left? Well, we were really drunk and the next thing we remember is that we were making out. Everything that happened after that just increased our confusion. But we knew we were in love," Kathryn smiled at her fiancée.

"We got engaged the night Agastya..." Laurel did not complete her sentence intentionally. I was not ready to face the truth that he was gone. "I swear we both wanted to tell you."

"But the circumstances weren't right."They were already finishing each other's sentences.

I was furious. I had not expected them to hide something so big for so long from me. "Get out," I ordered.

"Essie, stop being so irrational and listen to me. This is not right." But I was not to hear anything that she or Laurel had to say.

"Get the hell out!" I yelled and they did.

"We love you Essie," I heard Laurel whisper through the door.

I missed my Agastya. If he had been with me, nothing of this kind would have happened. He would've taken care of me and helped me keep my sanity, which seemed lost without him.

***

"Essie," Jean approached me. "Agastya would've wanted you to give the elegy."

"I can't. I don't have the strength to do that. I'm sorry."

"Please Estella, he loved you so much and you were the last of our family who was with him." She called me her family. But I still was not ready.

So I denied her request.

It was hard to believe that I was at the funeral of the man I was going to marry. My heart felt so crushed, my soul so comatose and my body so feeble. I was scared to be there with all those people. They were all looking at me and whispering 'Poor girl' to themselves. I was the girl whose love had died. I wanted to yell at them. Tell them they were wrong and that he was still alive. He was there with me, holding my hand and smiling as the way he always did. But what good would that lie have done?

I sat beside Jean and Daniela. Everyone there had loved Agastya dearly, especially his family. They all were as miserable as I was but somehow their concentration was on making me feel better. I wanted to return the favor and help them too. I dreadfully wanted to give them hope. But I was hopeless myself. My life had ended with his death. I was not making things worse; that was enough.

"Agu, I miss you. It's so hard to believe you're not with us anymore," Daniela was struggling to complete her words. "I remember when we were little; we used to play together a lot. He would be my personal bodyguard and I was the queen. And he would always say, 'Hang on Your Highness; I will taste this food first. It might be poisoned.' And I would let him do that just because he called me Your Highness. But he would eat everything in the name of tasting." Everyone laughed a little. "I need you to come back and taste my food again. I promise, that this time, I will not shout at you at all – I promise." Her husband rushed to hold her as she started to break down. He got her off the stage and sat her back down.

Jean held my hand and looked at me with tears gushing down her cheeks. "Please?" And I couldn't refuse her any more. I nodded to her and it made her smile.

I got on the stage and took out the note I had kept with me. I already knew that if his mother persisted, I wouldn't be able to refuse anymore. I did not know what to say, but that note had enough written on it to tell everyone what he had been to me.

Before I could say anything, I turned back and looked at the portrait of him. His smile was enough to give me a reason to live. "I did not know Agastya all my life. I existed before I met him and I exist after; this happening. But that small part of my life that I spent with him, it was my eternity. I literally lived in those months he was by my side, holding my hand, looking at me and randomly saying how beautiful I was. I'm sorry I don't have much to say about him. But I do have something he wrote for me. I hope it'll show you how exquisite he was."

Someday the world will be falling apart;

And the beings will be perishing in fear.

I'll hear the melody of your beating heart,

And will hold you tightly, to keep you near.

We will lie right there, as you hold my hand,

Your mesmerizing eyes will make me sigh.

The ground beneath will feel as soft as sand,

I promise I will never ever let the love die.

I'll pull you closer, wishing time to pause,

You will kiss me softly, and nest in my arms

I'll be the happiest man, whoever there was

For you are, better luck than any fluky charm.

When all the hopes of existence will be gone

My love, hold me snugly and quickly hide.

And I will be there always in some form,

Even if my body is lifeless by your side

***

"I love you Agastya. And I forever will."

Estella was lying on her bed in darkness. She had not moved for around five hours, listening to the songs Agastya sang for her. Her phone was constantly vibrating, but she declined every call. She looked her phone's screen when she received a text. Jay had called her seven times.

'I'm waiting outside Estella,' the text read.

She looked out the window and saw him standing against his car. For the first time,they were in reversed positions. She was up at the window looking down at him and he was outside in the cold night. She wanted to judge him the way she thought he judged her. She did not know that Jay had never judged her for dedicating a ritual to the one she loved. He, on the contrary, was jealous of her. He wished to do something as she had done for the one he loved. If only he wouldn't remember how it all had really ended.

Jay suddenly looked up and Estella ducked so that he couldn't see her. After a minute when she lifted her head up, he was not there anymore. She looked everywhere but he was nowhere to be found.

"I'm outside this door Estella," she was startled when she heard him say that from outside her door. She did not want him to see that it was Agastya's apartment. Agastya's belongings were all over the place, exactly as he had kept them.

"I'll be out in a minute." She was freaking out a little.

"Okay then. I'm waiting."

Jay had never done something to cheer someone up; especially a student. His life comprised only of Aarav. But somehow, he wanted to do something nice for her. He just had an urge to pull her out of her misery or perhaps drown in it with her. He had not realized that he was starting to think of Estella more than he was supposed to, but he had an inklingabout it.

That night, Opera's had a new singer. People were excited about it because he was a student of Jay's and the professor was there for the first time to hear someone sing.

"Professor, why are we here?" Estella asked Jay as they entered the bar.

"A student of mine really wanted me to hear him sing. He invited me here tonight," Jay replied. But then he remembered that he did not explain why she was there with him. "And because I wanted to make it up to you."

"Fine, I'll go get something to drink." Estella took off her coat and went to the bar.

Jay looked at her as she ordered a whiskey for herself. Estella Aurora Hudson, the girl whose fiancée had died. What was in her that made him so curious to get to know her more? Who was she that made him want to take her out that night?

He got off his seat and went up to her. "Estella" He tapped her shoulder. As soon as she turned around he held her in his arms. "You're not alone. I promise I'm with you. I will do anything to make you feel better. Just have faith in me please. I won't let you down."

Estella held him back and started to cry. "I have been waiting for you to say that to me Jay. Please help me, please," she wept.

"Are you going to take the glass or not sir?" Estella asked the zoned-out Jay. He was hallucinating, but about her. It was the second time that he was thinking of her. At that moment, Jay realized everything he had to. The girl standing in front of him with a clumsy ponytail and no makeup was something more than just a student to him.

She sat down with him and then the singer came on stage. "Hello everyone, I'm Saransh Shah and first of all, a special mention to the amazing Professor Jay Malhotra,who is here." Everyone applauded but the professor was busy in his thoughts. "Okay then, hope you like it."

Bright red dress you'll wear and a

Ring on your finger with the

Words written "I belong to you"

And you'll forever be mine

Oh yes, babe it's a sign

We're one of the lucky few

'Cause not everyone

Finds love so pure

Not everyone
Says, "I'm forever yours"
So come along this journey with me
Of love and joy and you'll see
That I'll take care of you
Take my hand and believe in me
With the smiles I promise you'll see
That I'll take care of you
I promise. Yes I do!
Soon we will be a family,
Living in love happily
With our little princess smiling
I'll give you all the finest things,
Take you away on pair of wings
Catch you when you'll be falling.
'Cause you're my love
And my life
Nothing's more important
Than to make you my wife
So come along this journey with me
Of love and joy and you'll see
That I'll take care of you
Take my hand and believe in me
With the smiles I promise you'll see

That I'll take care of you

I promise. Yes I do!

Everyone applauded with delight. The only person who did not like the song at all was Estella. She was reminded so much of what had happened in her past that she couldn't even bear to stay there any longer.

"I have to go," she got up and so did Jay.

"I'll drop you off." But before he could say anything else, she was already walking outside.

"Estella!" Jay tried to stop her.

"Sir, please let me go. I'm really very uncomfortable with all of this." Jay wanted to reply but he felt embarrassed by her words.

So he let her go.

"Double bourbon please." He returnedinto the bar in an irritated mood.

"Thank you for coming here today sir. It really meant a lot to me," Saransh approached him.

"Your song was nice; you're really talented Mr. Shah. And thank you for letting me bring one of my colleagues with me." Jay tipped his glass back and gulped down his bourbon in a single swallow.

"Oh, that's okay professor. As soon as you told me it was Estella Hudson, I couldn't have said no. I know she's been writing the annual plays for two years. That's a big deal. Where is she now by the way?"

Jay did not reply to that. He was furious with Estella for leaving without giving a legitimate reason.

"Remember your question the other day Mr. Shah?" Jay asked him and he nodded. "The thing is you cannot fix someone who is broken. You need to shatter yourself as much as they have, to show them that you're not just helping them, they're helping you. It's a kind of deception that you need to do to finally fix the person who is beyond repair. You know just, immerse yourself in the same despondency that they are in and I promise you, things will start to seem better," Jay said. "That's what I feel."

Saransh did not let Jay know that the person he wanted to fix was the girl he was in love with, Estella Hudson. He had been in love with her for a long time but the only difference was, she was his mentor's girlfriend. Agastya had been as amazing a music teacher as he had been a human being. And of course, the one with her, his Estella, she was beyond godliness.

Saransh was about to say something when Jay got a call from Aarav. "Not now Aarav, I'm not in the mood to talk."

"Jay, it's about Estella. She jumped in front of a car and is getting operated right now in Santé. Come as soon as possible."

Chapter – 11

How a Life Turns Into a Nightmare

[Autumn '08]

Jay was at Oxford University. He had achieved something that some people can only dream of. The child inside him continued to admire the wonder of architecture and the intellect that went into it. The faculty was very interested in him. And why wouldn't they be? His humble nature was as fascinating to them as was his academic performance.

As much as he loved being there as the apple of everyone's eyes, Jay's heart was still with his Viola. They would talk or video call for hours, regardless of the time difference. She would ask him constantly how he was and he would just smile knowing that she loved him so much.

"You stopped writing?"she asked him one evening on the video call.

"I don't know. I get really tired," he replied. "My muse isn't with me. Otherwise I would never stop."

He saw her smile, the one he always loved. "Your muse is always with you." She touched her computer screen.

"Then I'll write,"he smiled back.

"Good. Now I'm going to sleep. And I hope I'll find something when I'll get up." She was really excited. It's easy to love someone who looks attractive, but it's beautiful to love someone who is pure at heart and shows his sensuality through their work.

"I love you Viola. Sleep well."

"I love you my Jay Malhotra. Miss me."

The next morning when she woke up, she got an email from Jay. She jumped with happiness. Her boyfriend had kept his promise to her.

"With love, to the love of my life"

I don't know what it will take

To have you in my arms again;

Babe you really are my better half,

So come to turn this cry into a laugh.

No, I can't live without you this way,

I need you here with me right away;

I just wish this world was a smaller place,

So we'd be able to cuddle and embrace.

I hate this long distance so very much,

Maybe destiny's taking out an old grudge

Because I don't deserve this punishment,

Oh God, listen to these words of sentiment.

I'm going crazy being so far from you,

You don't say it out loud but you yourself too

Hate these hard moments of being so lonely,

Want to relive our time and stay with me only.

I can't look at your pictures forever,

And can't keep just texting as it will never

Be as equal to looking into your eyes,

As they seem like heaven in disguise.

So I'm waiting for you to come back here,

As our hearts are desperate to get near

Each other and feel that love again,

If I waited any longer, I'd go insane.

I just want to hold your beautiful hand in

Mine and caress it softly as I always did,

Just touch your blissful lips with mine,

And tell you all those mesmerizing lines

That I wrote or thought of for my muse;

Telling you 'I love you' isn't at all new,

But it'll have a new meaning and sound,

When I'll say it while swaying, you around.

Viola had tears in her eyes. She missed her Jay even more. But her smile was an assurance that she knew he loved her as much as she loved him. Her days were not passing as good as she had thought they would. Though she had started working in the laboratory of SantéHospital as a researcher, which paid her more than enough, but like the one she loved, her heart was not with her.

Weeks passed and they missed each other even more. One evening, when Viola returned from work, her watchman gave her a letter.

She applauded with delight. The only person who her Jay.

The meaning of my existence,

My Viola,

Hope you're doing better than I am as my nights and days feel meaningless without your hand in mine. The only thing I am interested in doing here is counting the days, hours and minutes left to see you again in flesh.

Oh this distance, no matter how much we talk – it just keeps showing its affect. I cannot take this thought that you're not physically with me out of my mind.

I just wish you could somehow send me the way you smell tonight or mark your eyeliner on theshirt that I'm wearing right now. If not any of those, then just do me this favor and keep smiling and saying 'I love you' as do you whenever I close my eyes.

You know, with every breath you take there, the craving in my heart to hold you in my arms, increases. I want to breathe the air you exhale, I want to see my reflection in your eyes, I want to hear my name from your lips and I want those arms of yours to hold me tightly and hide me from the world.

My love, this world that we're living in right now isn't the place for us. The world we live in when we are in each other's arms, that's the world we deserve. All I can say is that… can't wait to see you again.

I love you the most, keep being this perfection that you are.

All and only yours my moon,

Your man

Jay got a call from her instantly. "I guess you got the surprise?" he asked with excitement.

"Baby," Viola was crying, "Just come back soon. I miss you so much. I've never had longer days. Every hour without you here seems like a year. You are in my routine, please come back soon."

With those words, Viola touched Jay's soul. He was extremely restless and enthusiastic to see her too. "I tell you what, I'll come back for my birthday and we will celebrate it together. Is that okay?"

She agreed. It was the best idea Jay could've proposed.

[Autumn '08]

Love strengthens over time. But distance and time together can overpower the power of love. Something similar happened to Jay and Viola. His concentration was divided in his research and her. But hers seemed to have completely disappeared. Their conversations which used to last for an hour, was now limited to 10–15 minutes. He would ask her if something was wrong, but she wouldn't say anything. Jay was going insane with confusion so he did what he did best. He wrote.

My Beautiful Life,

My Viola,

It is so cold everywhere. I am starting to feel icy from inside. My lips ask me why they aren't touching yours; my fingers ask me why they aren't intertwined with yours, my eyes ask why they aren't looking in yours and my heart wants to know why it isn't close to your heartbeat. I just smile and say "Soon."

This year is coming to an end and I still cannot think of a moment that I was happy prior to meeting you. Falling in love with you was involuntary and baby, trust me when I say, it's the best happening of my existence. I can't stop smiling at the fact that you are all and only mine. I desire to find words to describe my emotions but unfortunately there are none at this moment.

My every thought begins and ends withyou; with a hope to be in your arms as soon as possible. In my heart I feel a melody being played sometimes and I realize it is your beautiful voice telling me that you want to see me soon too. These beliefs keep me happy and make my day brighter.

In the end I would just tell you that I am yearning to cup your face with my hands and touch your mesmerizing lips with mine. I want to feel whole again as I feel when you tell me you love me so much. And never worry about your Jay, it may get colder, but my heart conjures your touch andmakes my body stay warm with your love.

Take care of yourself for me.

All and only yours my sunlight,

Your man

Jay was hoping to get her reply. He waited for hercall for hours in the hope she would call and say something romantic. And then his phone's notification tune rang.

"I'm tired so I'm going to sleep. Goodnight, love you." That's all she had written.

He quickly called her up before she could go to sleep.

"Jay, I'm really sleepy."

"It'll take just a minute I promise. Did you get the letter I sent you?" he asked with hope in his heart.

"Yeah that letter reminded me, I don't think you should come in December." Jay's heart felt like it had dropped to his stomach.

"But why, I thought you wanted to meet me."

"I am but I'm really busy with work and we're on a breakthrough. I need time. We can meet some other time and talk about things. Anyways, I'll talk to you tomorrow. I'm basically sleeping on my phone," Viola seemed cold.

Jay was starting to get irritated. He did not know what things they needed to talk about… It was not like they were breaking up or going through a rough patch. He understood that the distance had started to create problems between them.

"Okay. But will you do me a favor? On my birthday, go to the cherry blossom tree near the lake, the place where we danced together that night and just, miss me. Can you do that?" The little hope he had was begging Viola to say yes.

She was quiet for some time "Sure. I promise. Goodnight and, I love you Jay."

Her last words made Jay feel alright. And though he had just asked her to be at the lake on his birthday, he had different plans.

[Winter '08]

"Aarav, I have reached the airport. Are you here to pick me up?" I called him as soon as my flight landed. It was supposed to be a surprise for Viola.

"Oh I'm sorry Jay; I've been trying to come to you but I'm stuck in the restaurant's construction."

"It's alright man. Just meet me at the Reindeer Gardens when you're free. I'll be there." Jay was really excited and the reason was not his birthday, but the fact that he was going to finally meet the love of his life again.

"Okay, I've to go pick Jay up in an hour. Do you think he would like the decorations and everything Amy?" Aarav asked Amelia. Both of them were planning a surprise birthday party for Jay. But that was not the only important occasion of that day. They were also celebrating the fact that Amelia was going to get a new heart. But it was a secret that they had kept from Jay.

"Of course Aarav, don't worry about it. Trust me; this is going to turn into the best birthday ever," Amy replied excitedly. Her health had really gotten worse in the last few weeks. It was the perfect time for her to get a new heart otherwise she couldn't survive longer.

Jay had not told Aarav or anyone else about his plans. He bought flowers for Viola and was waiting near the lake. He looked charismatic in the suit that he had bought specially for that day.

He called Viola but she did not pick up so he left her a voicemail. "I didn't want to ruin the surprise, but I'm here baby. I'm at the lake where I requested you to be. I think you're running late. It's okay. Just come here as soon as possible. I love you so much." His smile was wide with happiness.

An hour passed and there was no sign of her. Jay's excitement was waning. He sent her another voicemail. "Hey baby, you're coming right? I'm waiting here. Please come soon. I love you and I'm eagerly waiting for you."

After two hours of waiting, Jay's became irritated. "Viola, what on earth are you doing? Please come here. I'm dying of the wait." A part of Jay was scared that something bad had happened to her. But he needed to stay positive.

And then finally his phone rang. He pulled it out with his heart throbbing but it wasn't Viola.

"I wish you a very happy birthday Jay," Amelia spoke.

"Thank you Amy. That's really nice of you to remember," Jay said to her coldly.

"What happened? Why do you seem upset?" As soon as Amelia asked Jay that question, his irritation reached a new level.

"Let me be Amelia. I'm fine."

"You don't seem fine at all Jay. Tell me what happened?"

"Stop asking me these stupid questions. I'm not in the mood." It was the first time Jay had spoken to her rudely.

"Hey, I'm just trying to help you."

"Oh yes? Well I'm just trying to stay the hell away from you so let me freaking be." He hung up the call. He knew that Amelia was really upset with his words but at that moment he was getting desperate to see Viola.

"Hey man what happened?" Aarav arrived to pick him up.

"I'm waiting for Viola. She was supposed to be here but she isn't yet."

Aarav felt a little awkward. Jay did not even smile when he saw him. They had met after six months and Jay acted like it had been just a few hours.

"It's okay dude. Come I'll take you home. We'll celebrate your birthday," Aarav kept pleading with Jay, but Jay refused to budge.

"Aren't you Jay Malhotra?" someone tapped Jay's shoulder.

"I am," Jay recognized the man. "You're Akshat, right? Amelia's doctor." Jay and Aarav shook hands with him.

"Well yeah, but right now I'm officially a groom," he laughed.

"Congratulations to you. Oh and this person, is the birthday boy," Aarav pointed to Jay.

"Oh a very happy birthday to you Jay, what are you doing here?"

"Waiting for someone. Unfortunately she's a bit late," Jay replied sadly.

"That's disappointing. Why don't you come to my wedding? Stay for the ceremony. If your 'someone' arrives, you could come back here. I'm sure they'd call you," Akshat suggested.

"That's a great idea. I always love wedding ceremonies," Aarav held Jay's arm. "We would love to be a part of it."

Jay reluctantly agreed and they went into the chapel with Akshat.

They sat at the back. Fortunately Jay was already looking like a guest at a wedding and no one could ever argue with Aarav's choice of clothes. He always wore everything that made him look like a gentleman.

"This is insane. We need to leave. What if Viola arrives and waits for me there?" Jay whispered to Aarav.

"That's fine Jay, stop being a baby. What did Akshat say? If she comes, she'll call you or text you or at least shout your name at the top of her lungs. One of those options should work."

"I still don't think…" Jay's heart skipped a beat when he saw the woman in the front row. It was Viola's mother. He instantly turned to Aarav and held his arm. Before he could say anything, he heard the music that marked the arrival of the bride.

Jay's heart stopped when he saw Viola as the bride. His whole body felt dead and his soul was in pieces. He clutched the diamond ring he had bought for her tightly;it was in his pocket. Aarav was startled as well – his eyes popped out of their sockets, but more importantly, he was focused on his friend.

The bride passed Jay without noticing him. But she had only walked a step when she stopped and looked to her right. Her eyes were filled with shame and pain. She just kept standing there looking at Jay, who had lost the meaning of his life as soon as he had seen her.

Viola's mother saw her standing and when she realized the reason, she got really nervous. She knew that he would do something ruin the wedding. She quickly hurried up to Viola and escorted her to her groom and ran back to Jay.

"Listen to me Jay Malhotra, this wedding is really important to Viola and me. She is marrying a successful colleague of hers who has a respected job and isn't from a family of psycho serial killers," Jay turned to her with tears in his eyes. "If you love this girl, you won't say a word. Let her be happy. That's what should matter to you." She whispered to him while gripping his arm with her nails.

Jay stood there, lifeless, watching the love of his life getting married to someone else. He prayed for her to turn around once but she didn't.

"Viola Irene Harris, do you take Akshat Gupta as your lawfully wedded husband in sickness and in health?" the priest asked her. And she replied with the worst answer that she could've given.

"I do."

"Akshat Gupta, do you take Viola Harris as your lawfully wedded wife in sickness and in health?"

"I do," he replied with a smile.

"If any of you have reasons why they shouldn't get married, speak now or forever hold your peace."

Viola's mother was praying for this part to go smoothly. "I object!" Jay yelled. "This girl, she loves me and I love her."

Everyone in the chapel was surprised by the sudden happenings.

"Please Viola, don't do this to me. You know you love me, not him. Let's run away." He approached them but before he could say anything else, he was knocked out by a furious Akshat.

"Jay, what the hell is wrong with you?" Aarav punched Jay's arm. "This is your chance to say something – when the priest asks if anyone has an objection." Jay was hallucinating. It was the first time that he had been imagining an event in broad daylight.

"If any of you have reasons why they shouldn't get married, speak now or forever hold your peace." The priest asked the question again.

Jay was about to say something when Viola turned her face and their eyes met. He asked her through his eyes if she was in love with him. But her expressions showed him the truth. She signaled to him not to say anything.

And he agreed.

Aarav wanted to say a lot too. His best friend's trust and heart were broken ruthlessly and he felt helpless. If Jay did not say anything, it was not in his place to say anything.

"Go home Jay," Aarav gave Jay the car keys. "I'll be at the restaurant. Oh and Amy's has arranged for a surprise party. I'll tell her everything, don't worry."

Aarav left for his restaurant. He was in shock too. He had trusted her with Jay's heart and she had taken it for granted.

Jay did not hear a word, or rather chose not to hear. The only thing he could see was Viola's face, signaling him not to say a word. All he could hear was her voice when she said 'I do.' It was something that was meant to be just for him. Or that's what he was hoping it would be. The only question remaining in his mind was why she had done that to him. He tried to think of numerous answers, but couldn't come up with a logical one.

He reached his apartment,expecting to see an angry Amelia. But he was damaged. He couldn't think of anything other than the nightmare he had been through.

As soon as he unlocked the door, he found Amelia lying on the floor…dead.

He rushed to her and tried his best to bring her back to life.

"Amy, no, you're okay Amy. Please come back to me. It's all going to be okay. Come back to me please Amy!" He called for an ambulance and called Aarav, hoping some miracle would make her okay. He looked around and the banner read 'It is Jay's birthday', but the heartbreaking thing was what was written beneath it. 'And Amy's getting a new heart'.

After trying for some time, Jay gave up. Amelia had died and it was his fault. Her phone was in her hand and the last call on it was to Jay. She had had a stroke when he had yelled at her. She was too fragile to live through it.

Jay's tears did not stop. He had lost everything in a span of minutes. He lost the love of his life, the one he wanted to be with. And he lost his soulmate, the one he was supposed to be with.

It might have been the end of Jay's happiness. But his depression was just born.